I0547152

Patrick Gloutney

The Hidden Island

Stonecroft Publishing

Create Space Edition
Copyright © 2015 by Patrick Gloutney

ISBN: 978-0-9947251-1-0

This book is licensed for your personal enjoyment only. This book may not be re-sold or given away to other people. If you would like to share this book with another person, please purchase an additional copy for each recipient. If you're reading this book and did not purchase it, or it was not purchased for your use only, then please return to Amazon.com and purchase your own copy. Thank you for respecting the hard work of this author.

All characters appearing in this work are fictitious. Any resemblance to real persons, living or dead, is purely coincidental.

No part of this book may be reproduced or transmitted in any form or by any means, electronic or mechanical, including photocopying, recording, electronic transmission, or by any storage and retrieval system, without written permission from the author.

Cover photo © iStock
Cover design © 2015, Patrick Gloutney

Patrick Gloutney

To my grandfather, the late Pierre Gloutney, who was always so proud and
supportive of me in my endeavors.

The Hidden Island

There is no stronger army than the one fighting for its freedom.—

Unknown

Patrick Gloutney

Serenidad

The island was discovered by a wealthy American biologist named Angus MacDiarmid seventy-five years ago. Angus landed on the shore after spotting what appeared to be a new plant species. He later brought a small group of scientists to study the plant more thoroughly. After extensive research and testing they discovered that the plant contained a chemical that, when boiled with seawater, produced an eco-friendly diesel fuel replacement that could help cut transport costs around the world. However, they never fully understood why the plants grew only on the one island. Angus invited more scientists—as well as people he knew—to come work on this island, providing them with housing, food, and good wages on the condition that the island's location remain secret. Most of these people willingly took the opportunity to start a new life.

The primary reason for bringing people out to the island was to make it completely self-sufficient. As more people came from all over the world, Angus developed an agriculture industry, education and, most prominently, a defensive industry. Angus knew that other nations would want to try to take the island by force if necessary, so to help protect the island's inhabitants, he founded a Navy that became the major employer on the island. Angus was thrilled when the scientists on the island discovered that the steam created from the boiling process created a cloud layer that could prevent aircraft from taking pictures of the island. They soon made this into a "cloaking" system and ran it twenty-four hours a day. After perfecting the alternate diesel fuel, they established trading agreements with China, Russia, most of Europe, and only recently with the USA. They always kept their location hidden by delivering their product to the purchasers. The island and Angus made millions from the fuel trade allowing an economy to develop on the island and soon Angus was no longer paying out of his own pocket. After the economy established itself, people began to want to bring their families to the island. Angus allowed this and the population of the island grew to 7,000. However, the inhabitants of the island never left a large carbon footprint as the natural state of the island was what supported them. In ten years, Angus had created a peaceful, completely separate environment in which people could live and work in good conditions and complete safety. People weren't trapped on the island. If they wanted to leave, they could hitch a ride on the island tanker to the mainland or have one of the large aircraft fly them out. Most people stayed, though. Only a few left and some even went to a university or a college and then came back with proper experience for their industry. Angus lived on and ran the island for thirty years before he died and passed the baton to his son who later retired after a long term, passing the position to his son, Russell. It was paradise for many until...

Under the Radar

Africa Air flight 2367

Jeff looked nervously at his co-pilot. What if this didn't work? What if the controllers didn't believe him? What if they couldn't get below the radar cover? He decided to do what the organization wanted him to do.

"Mayday. Mayday. This is Africa Air flight 2367. We have a fire on board in our upper rear cargo compartment." He said this calmly into the microphone. He could feel sweat running down the back of his neck. He was holding the control column of his Military Boeing 747 Combine so tightly that his knuckles had turned white. He checked his squawker to make sure that he was transmitting an airliner code. He had just sent a fake Mayday to an experienced controller. Would they notice how nervous he was or would they notice the absence of the crackling of fire or the absence of circuit breakers popping?

"Roger," came the response. "Africa Air flight 2367 squawk 7700. Would you like vectors to nearest airport?"

Jeff let his shoulders relax before he responded. They believed there was a fire on board. "Yes, we would," he replied.

"Roger that. What type of aircraft are you flying?"

"A Boeing 747 Combine. We have forty-one percent fuel."

"Roger that. Turn left, heading 260."

"Roger, Africa Air flight 2367 turning left onto heading 260."

Now came the hard part. He had to put the plane into a left turn and then he had to roll the aircraft and dive. Then at 2,000 feet he would pull hard on the control column to level off at a hundred feet or so. That was the plan. No doubt about it, it was a great plan except for the fact that he had to pull a 4.65 G maneuver to get the plane level. He was about to find out if his plane could do it or not.

"Jeff. *Jeff!* They said to turn fifteen seconds ago. They're going to wonder why we haven't turned."

Jeff was so deep in thought that his co-pilot Leo's voice startled him. Leo was a small man to be flying the 747. His feet just reached the rudder petals. But he was one of the best co-pilots with whom Jeff had ever flown. Jeff put the 747 into its turn. Three seconds later he rolled the aircraft and it started to dive.

"Mayday! Mayday! This is Africa Air flight 2367. We have lost control of our aircraft and we are di—"

At that point Leo killed the radio. Jeff let the aircraft fall to 2,000 feet and then pulled back hard on the control column. He could feel the 4.65 G push his body into his seat. He held his breath and waited for the plane to break apart.

Cairo

Aly Hakbare glanced at the clock on the wall of the old rundown building. It was 9:30 PM. The plane was supposed to have landed in Cairo at 2:30 AM. He turned to the members of the mercenary group called the Free Army Republic, or FAR, and started his presentation.

"Good evening, ladies and gentleman. Exactly five minutes ago, a Boeing 747 Combine declared an emergency. This emergency was simply a distraction for the plane to be able to dip below radar cover. If all goes well, in five hours—at 0230—it will touch down in Cairo. On board are military weapons which will be used to help us take the island."

Everyone in the room knew the significance of what he was saying. They knew about a small island in the Pacific Ocean, code named Foxtrot India, that had created a product that brought them great wealth—and which the FAR intended to take. No one in the FAR knew the history of the island or what its military defenses were, so Aly was drafted as a civilian to make sure that the FAR's small army would have the weapons and supplies they needed. On top of Aly's mission, other members of the FAR had turned to the islanders while they were away from Foxtrot India to study at US schools.

Aly looked around the room and saw General Ihejirika shaking his head. "Problem, General?"

"Yes," the General responded with a hint of concern in his voice.

"There is. How is the plane supposed to dip below radar cover? And how is it supposed to do a seven-hour-and-thirty-minute flight in five hours?"

"The aircraft will roll and dive, report that they lost control of their aircraft, they'll pull a 4.65 G maneuver, then fly at MAX speed all the way to Cairo." Aly watched Ihejirika the whole time he spoke to see the look of concern transform into a fire of anger in the General's eyes.

"Who's flying the plane?" Ihejirika asked calmly.

"Two of our best."

Ihejirika's face stiffened and it appeared that he was about to bite off Aly's head. "Are you nuts? No Boeing 747 has ever survived a 4.65 G maneuver before. Never! And now you've sent our best pilots out there— with millions of dollars of military weapons I might add—to be destroyed when the aircraft breaks apart?" The anger in Ihejirika's eyes was now a hot blazing inferno.

"The aircraft will not break up. It will survive—"

Ihejirika cut him off. "How do you know that? Did you modify the aircraft?"

"We did not." Aly could feel all eyes on him, like missiles locked onto a target. What was I thinking? Ihejirika's right. The aircraft doesn't have a good chance of surviving.

"Well, Aly?"

Aly had to keep calm. He had to. "I guess we'll just have to hope for the best." He knew his voice was calm but could see that Ihejirika was not happy. He looked like someone had just crashed his favorite car into a tree.

"We will just have to hope for the best? You truly are nuts. You've just sent two good and valuable pilots to their deaths and all you have to say is that we will just have to hope for the best." His voice was rough and deep with rage.

"We didn't think of what the high stress of the maneuver would do to the plane," Aly said, now annoyed with the General. "I will take full responsibility for what happens."

"That won't change what *does* happen. What about the families of these men? What about all the—"

"I said that I will take full responsibility for what happens. And that's my final word on the matter. Do you understand me?" Aly waited for a response but none came. "Do you understand me, General?"

"Yes, *sir*," Ihejirika said, clearly not pleased.

"Good. Now this meeting is adjourned." Aly watched as the men and women filed out of the office. "Not you, Mr. Aisle."

Aband Aisle was a tall, dark, thin man with wavy hair and just a faint trace of a moustache and a beard on his face. "Yes, sir." He approached Aly.

"What have I done? Ihejirika's right. I have sent two men to their deaths."

"No you haven't, sir. I know these pilots. They can land a plane with only one-and-a-quarter wings. Even if the plane's damaged, sir, they can land it safe here in Cairo." He made direct eye contact with Aly. "By the way, what's the flight path?" His eyes shifted away. "If you don't mind me asking."

"You must know that that information is highly classified at this time." Aly received a nod from Aband. "Now go home, Aband. Get some sleep. I need you here at 0215 sharp. Understood?"

"Yes, sir!" Aband saluted and quickly turned and walked out of the room. Shortly after, Aly did the same. He needed sleep, too. But how could he? All he could think about was the 747 Combine and the two pilots flying her.

Africa Air flight 2367

All the alarms were sounding. Jeff had to pull up the nose of the 747 to keep the #3 and #4 engines out of the water. He heard the STALL alarm and had to lower the nose to increase the air speed of the aircraft before it slipped from the sky. Things hadn't gone according to plan at all. The aircraft was taking much more time to level off than Jeff had expected and they were now literally skimming the water. Jeff had to get the plane to 100 feet or their engines would dip into the water and take the whole plane with them. He glanced at his air speed indicator: 160 knots.

Oh man. They were lucky they were still in the air. He pushed the throttles to MAX and waited for the air speed indicator to rise. But nothing happened.

"Leo! Air speed indicator's malfunctioned. How about yours?" This came out louder than he wanted it to.

"Same here. The backup as well. The maneuver must have knocked them out of whack." Leo was clearly nervous.

Of course he's nervous. We've lost our air speed indicators. Without them, they had no way of knowing how fast they were going and if they didn't know that, they could fall from the sky without even a hint from the aircraft. Jeff took a huge chance and brought the nose of the 747 up and then... Nothing. No alarms. Just the soft clicking of the altimeter needle moving to the right. The 747 climbed gracefully through the air for the second it took to get to a hundred feet.

"Altimeters are working, Leo. Good." He leaned back in his seat, trying to relax. "Do a systems check."

"I'll check the auto pilot first." Leo turned the TEST knobs.

"Call them out as you go." It seemed that no matter how hard he tried, Jeff just couldn't relax.

"Giros 1 and 2 are good, but gyro 3 is down." Leo seemed very calm. Jeff was amazed at how his co-pilot could go from nervous to calm in just two seconds.

"Autopilot back-up computer is OK," Leo continued, "but the main one is damaged beyond repair. Also the number two GPS link is down. But we can still fly without it. The main fuel pumps are offline. We are right now running on secondary and the center A.D.I. is jammed even though its gyro is working." Leo stopped to readjust the computer so he could continue.

All these failures, Jeff thought. I wouldn't be surprised if an engine falls off next.

"The cabin's electrical bus is out, so there's no lights back there. All the engine gauges are down. Hydraulic system two is down. I'll go back and check the wings."

Jeff waited for what he hoped was going to be good news. Had the wings been damaged?

"Good news, Jeff," Leo called out excitedly. "There's no structural damage to the wings at all." He re-entered the cabin and sat down. "Finally. Something's working."

Jeff could feel himself relax. Even with all the failures, they could still fly the plane. "Any more failures or problems, Leo?" Jeff asked, expecting another long list.

"Not that I can tell," Leo said with a hint of relief. "Except for the part about no airspeed,"

Jeff got tense again as soon as Leo mentioned the airspeed indicators. They were by far the most severe loss and, alone, could cause the plane to go for an unwanted swim.

"What time is it, Leo?" Jeff believed they were behind schedule.

"Um. 9:45 PM."

Jeff couldn't believe it. "Did you say its 9:45?"

"Yeah. Well it's 9:46 now. Why?"

"We're five minutes ahead of schedule. How can that be? The maneuver. All the failures... Heck. We don't even know what speed we're flying at and we're ahead of schedule." This puzzled Jeff.

"I don't know, Jeff. Maybe we're just that good?" Leo laughed, proud of himself.

"Nah, we aren't that good, we're just lucky," Jeff said, still very surprised. "I'm turning on the autopilot. Get ready to take control from the computer." Jeff leaned forward and turned the FLIGHT DIRC dial to AUTO.

The Hidden Island

Leo was there, his hands just a fraction of an inch from the yoke. After five minutes, he took his hands away and sat back in his seat.

"Better get comfortable, we have another four hours and forty-five minutes of flying time." Jeff leaned back in his own seat.

On board the *MV Halie*

"We should be at the crash site in two minutes," Captain Mjil said to Jehlie.

"Good," Jehlie responded. He grabbed the microphone and addressed the crew of the *MV Halie*.

"Good evening. We will be dumping wreckage into the ocean in an attempt to create the appearance of a crash site."

The *MV Halie* was the perfect ship for this job. It was a fishing vessel that was big enough to hold the wreckage of a 747 Combine and if anyone saw the vessel, they would just think it was going out fishing.

"We have reached the crash site," Captain Mjil said.

Jehlie grabbed the microphone again. "Start pushing the wreckage overboard and make sure the Black Boxes are tangled up in one of the tail section pieces."

Patase grabbed a piece of metal and pushed it off the deck of the *MV Halie*, then went to help with the engines which were mounted on rails welded to the deck of the *MV Halie*. Patase removed the straps that secured the mangled engines and an hydraulic piston pushed the engines over the edge of the vessel.

Patase walked across the deck to help with the last piece. It was part of the tail of the 747. It took half the crew to move it while the rest directed. As soon as they pushed the piece over, the crew headed back to their cabins. All except for Patase.

Why, he wondered. *Why are we doing this?* Just then he heard a high-pitched noise. Then he saw it. A trail of what seemed to be fire was flying low. He could see the water spreading apart from the force of the missile's engine, and he could see that *it was heading right for the* MV Halie! He grabbed his walkie-talkie and shouted into it.

"Missile off the stern! Turn the boat!"

The boat lurched to the right, nearly knocking him off his feet, but it was too late. The missile plowed into the side of the *MV Halie* sending Patase crashing into a pile of fishing nets. Then a second missile hit the fuel tanks and it was all over.

Cairo

"How did this happen?" Aly glared at each and every single person in the room. He had a large cup of coffee at his right side and a red folder on his left. He had been awakened from his sleep by a phone call. The man on the other end had informed him that the *MV Halie* had been shot by a missile. "Well Mr. Aisle?"

"We don't know, sir," Aband responded.

Aly could tell he was nervous. "Well, what *do* you know then? The position? The type of missile?"

"We don't know much, sir. But we do know that the vessel was finished with dumping the wreckage before it was hit."

"Sir. How are we to explain the boat sitting down on the bottom of the ocean right next to the 747 wreckage with explosives residue on it?" Ihejirika asked, obviously enraged.

"We could say that the 747 hit the *MV Halie* on the way down?" Aband offered.

"And the explosives residue?" Ihejirika demanded.

"I guess... I guess I don't know," Aband said.

Aly looked at Aband, whose cheeks were now bright red. "There's a lot of explosives residue in that water now after the South Africans did all their missile testing," he said, coming to Aband's rescue. "That's how we'll explain the missile that hit the *MV Halie*. The 747 wreckage is probably as full of residue as the *MV Halie* is right now."

"Right. We blame South Africa for the residue." Aband's smile was wide.

"No, not blame," said Aly. "We'll simply point out that there's a lot of explosives residue in those waters. We don't want to provoke the South Africans any further." He picked up his coffee. "Right now we have a very pressing matter on our hands, don't we?" He saluted the group with his cup. "The only people who know about our plane are in this room. So one of these people..." With his free arm, Aly made a grand sweeping motion across the room. "... is a traitor."

Africa Air flight 2367

Jeff waited until Leo sat down and fastened himself into his seat after his washroom break, then he did a quick instruments check. "How's our fuel, Leo?"

"Good. We're running a few pounds ahead."

"Better ahead than behind, I say." Both men laughed. It seemed odd, laughing in a situation like this, where they could fall out of the sky at any moment. And a millisecond later, a shudder ran through the aircraft.

"What was that?" As if in response to his question, he heard a loud bang and a high-pitched alarm. A red light began to flash. The right wing rose immediately. Jeff had to throw the yoke to the right to level the plane before it plunged into the ocean.

"What in the world just happened?" Jeff asked, holding the controls as if they would save him.

"Engine 4 RUNAWAY! We have to bring back power on engine 4," Leo responded at nearly a scream.

Jeff reached down and pulled #4's throttle back fifteen percent. The RPMs of the over-speeding engine dropped and the plane leveled off.

"Regulator must have gotten damaged in the maneuver."

After the plane leveled, Jeff did a sweep of his instruments, stopping at his engine gauges the longest even though they weren't working. "Any chance the other engines might do the same thing?"

"Um..." Leo shook his head. "I can't see all the engines being damaged the same way." He looked out the window at #3 and #4.

"Can we fly with this engine running or do we have to shut it down?" Jeff glanced at the fuel gauges.

"Well... The engine can still run. It's not going to tear itself apart if that's what you're thinking. The only problem is that we won't know how fast it's spinning. If we shut it down we might not have the fuel to make it to Cairo."

"It won't burn extra fuel?"

"No. Come on. You know that. What's wrong with you? The automatic injection system won't let it. Jeff, did you bump your head during the maneuver?"

I must have bumped my head before I volunteered for this operation, Jeff thought. "How long until we reach Cairo?"

"Two hours and twenty-eight minutes," Leo said, after glancing at his watch.

"Man, what have we gotten ourselves into this time, Leo?" He looked out the window at the sparkling black water rushing by a hundred feet below them. "Orders are that we can't be seen. Not by radar. Not by anybody standing on a beach—Wait a minute, who would be on a beach in the middle of the night?"

"You're right, Jeff. We're just following orders. That's all. If we die, they lose the plane, they lose all the equipment on board, and most importantly they lose the two best pilots they ever had."

"I doubt they'll think much of us if their millions of dollars of equipment end up sitting on the bottom of the ocean." His own words sent a chill down his spine.

"That's where you're wrong. I know one of the men in charge. So do you. He knows when we joined up we became loyal to the Free Army Republic so he'd care if something happened to us. I know it."

Jeff knew that Leo was trying to sound certain, but he knew he was thinking the same thing he was.

Gripen flight 12, lead aircraft

Kosie was watching the water rush by beneath his JSA 39 Gripen D. It seemed so peaceful—if one took away the roar from the GE F404 turbofan engine behind him. *This would be one of the most peaceful places on earth,* he thought as he watched a small fishing boat disappear from view. As he brought his eyes to the nose of the aircraft, he noticed what appeared to be a tail plane moving off at his ten o'clock. He glanced at his fuel gauges: three-quarters in each tank.

Plenty of fuel. I can go have a look at whatever that was and still make it to the base.

"Wingman, this is Leader. Do you copy? Over."

"This is Wingman. I copy."

"What is your fuel level?"

"A little less than three-quarters each tank," his Wingman replied.

"I thought I saw something off to our left."

"Then why don't we go have a look?"

Kosie's Wingman was always up for adventure and Kosie could understand why he was excited. So was Kosie. This would be their first time in actual combat if this turned out to be an intruder.

"All right, then. Follow my lead," Kosie said as he banked left toward the heading he thought the object had taken.. "Switching on radar. Do the same, Wingman. Let me know."

Patrick Gloutney

"Roger that, Leader."

It took a few minutes, but the two aircraft finally found what they were looking for. Kosie hit the identify button and a small transmitter/receiver in the nose of the aircraft sent out four radar pulses to determine the shape, size, heading, and type of aircraft. When Kosie got the response from the computer he sat back in his seat.

"A 747. A 747? What a waste of time and fuel to go chasing a 747."

"What's that, Leader?"

"Nothing, Wingman. Just muttering to myself." Kosie was disappointed that it had not been an intruder. He peered out the nose of the aircraft to try to see the plane, but it was too far off. He checked his radar setting. It was pointing down. Kosie was flying at a thousand feet. That meant the 747 was flying *below* a thousand.

What in the world is going on here? A 747 flying lower than a thousand feet in the middle of nowhere? His thoughts were interrupted by his Wingman's voice over the radio.

"Leader, this is Wingman. What kind of aircraft is that thing?"

"It's a 747." Kosie replied shaking his head.

"That's what I thought, too. But a 747?"

"Yeah. And the bigger problem is that it's flying really low. My guess is a hundred feet. Want to close the distance? Get a visual? Figure out what's going on?" When no reply came he looked out to see his Wingman drifting away. "Hey, we have the fuel to do it and we have weapons. If it *is* hostile, we can blow it out of the sky. If we don't blow him up we will definitely scare him."

"Yeah. Let's go scare this guy back to where he came from," Kosie's Wingman replied with a hint of disappointment in his voice.

Africa Air Flight 2367

Jeff passed through the door to the upper rear cargo compartment of the 747 Combine. The plane was so full of equipment that even the part of the plane that was normally for passengers was piled high. When he reached the back of the upper rear cargo compartment, he sat down to inspect the boxes. One of them was marked CLASSIFIED. Below that one was a box with

WARNING
HIGH EXPLOSIVES
HANDLE WITH CARE

What in the world are we carrying? A bullet hits one of these boxes and we could be blown out of the sky. He looked around again and realized that almost every box in the upper rear cargo compartment was marked the same. They all had explosives materials in them.

He rose and headed toward the front of the plane but stopped when he heard the whine of a supersonic jet engine. He ran to a window. What he saw made the hair on the back of his neck stand up. He immediately ran to the front of the plane and burst into the cockpit.

"Hey. What's wrong? You see a ghost or something?"

"There's two Gripen Ds out there."

"What? Where?" Leo tried to jump out of his seat to see where the two fighters were but the restraints pulled him back into his seat with a nasty jolt.

"Off the left wing tip." Jeff said, quickly sitting down and putting on his restraints as fast as his trembling hands would let him.

"Um... They aren't on the wing tip anymore," Leo said, pointing a trembling finger out the window behind Jeff.

Jeff turned around and then jolted back against his chair. The Gripen D was so close to the 747 cockpit that Jeff could clearly see the pilot motioning for them to change radio frequency to one-one-decimal-nine. Jeff looked farther to the left and he could clearly see the missiles mounted underneath the Gripen's wing. That's when he noticed the South African markings on its tail.

"They're South African." Jeff reached down to change the radio frequency to the requested one-one-decimal-nine then signaled that he'd complied with their request.

"What the heck are South Africans doing out here?"

"Unknown aircraft, this is Gripen flight 12 Leader. State why you are flying so low."

Jeff looked at Leo. "What do we tell them?"

"Well, we can't tell them the truth that's for sure. And if we stall too long the FAR will leave."

"Leo? You're a genius. That's it."

"What? I didn't suggest anything." Leo's frown of puzzlement almost made Jeff laugh.

"We'll tell them the truth." Before Leo could say anything Jeff cued the microphone.

"Gripen flight 12 this is unknown aircraft." As Jeff spoke he made a hand signal that he and Leo had invented for this very mission. It meant get ready to cut the radio. "We've been experiencing some problems with our aircraft and are unable to climb. We don't know our airspeed and are having some radio trouble. We may not be able to keep the radio working much lo—"

Jeff made his signal, Leo cut the radio, then Jeff reached down to push the throttles to MAX but when he realized they were already there, he brought the nose of the plane up to an unnatural angle then slipped it sideways.

Gripen flight 12, lead aircraft

Kosie yanked his Gripen hard to the right and did a complete circle around the 747 before he leveled off.

Well, that confirms the pilot's story, he thought, keeping an eye on the 747 to make sure he was a safe distance away from it.

"Wingman, this is Leader do you copy?" Kosie waited for a reply. When none came, he tried again. Kosie slowed his plane to come up on the other side of the 747 to find his Wingman. Kosie could feel the sweat run down his back. Lots and lots of sweat.

Calm down before you fill the whole cockpit up with sweat. Finally, when he looked out over the nose of his Gripen, he saw his Wingman off the left wing tip of the 747.

What is he doing? Why didn't he answer my radio transmission?

All of a sudden the left wing of the 747 shot up and hung there for a second. Kosie looked down at his Wingman who had drifted closer to the 747. Kosie looked back up at the wing of the 747 just as it started to fall back down. He watched in terror as his Wingman dove toward the water to avoid the 747's wing, only to have its own wing grab the water. The wing was torn off his Wingman's fuselage. In response to the lighter right side of the aircraft, the fighter immediately rolled to the left and then plunged into the ocean. Kosie looked back to the 747, then turned the WEAPONS SELECT dial to RADAR MISSILES and armed them. He pushed his throttles up and closed the distance between the two planes.

"Don't worry, friend. I will avenge you."

The distance between the two planes was closing fast. Kosie's Gripen D was well within the normal firing range of its missiles but Kosie wanted to get as close as possible to ensure a hit. A few seconds later he found himself slipping off to the side of the aircraft and in the same situation that his Wingman had been in. He cursed under his breath, reached down and fired a missile while at the same time jamming the throttles forward to full afterburner.

The missile launched off the wing of the Gripen, which quickly passed it. Confused by the small radar contact on the narrow edge of the wing of the 747, and the bigger radar contact of the Gripen D that had launched it, the missile changed target and followed the larger radar contact.

The missile alert alarm rang in Kosie's ear. He looked back to see his own missile on his own tail. He yanked the plane to the left and punched out four bundles of chafe from the rear ejector. This would normally paint a bigger radar image to confuse the missile, but Kosie knew the chafe wouldn't work. The missile, a new model programmed not to be confused by chafe, plowed into the plane's engine. The force of the explosion sent what remained of the Gripen into a step climb.

"Shot by my own missile! That has to be a world first," Kosie said aloud as he desperately tried to level the aircraft, but it was no use. All that was left of the Gripen was the cockpit and the two small wings at the front of the aircraft. The crippled Gripen slipped sideways and then fell to the ocean. Kosie never had a chance to eject. It had all happened too fast.

Kosie surfaced a few yards from where his plane had crashed and grabbed a piece of floating wreckage. He could see the 747 flying off in the distance. He looked up to see a flaming piece of wreckage falling toward him. He tried to swim but his legs wouldn't move.

Broken.

He cursed at the 747 and her crew as the flaming wreckage landed on him breaking his neck.

Africa Air Flight 2367

"Holy snapping turtles," Leo whooped. "That guy just blew himself out of the sky! OK, one down, one to go." He peered out the window to see where the other fighter had gone to.

"Don't bother looking, We got that one already."

"We did?" Leo said, still looking.

"When we did the wing up and wing down thing. I heard an explosion and then this guy comes up and flies in front of us with his own missile on his tail."

Jeff changed the topic. "Any chance, you think, the fighters could have radioed in our coordinates?"

"I don't think they had time to radio our position," Leo said in a mocking tone.

Jeff glanced down at his instruments. They were back on course and all was going well for the moment. "So, say they did radio in our position. How long do you think it'll take backup to get here?"

"Thirty minutes," Leo responded. "Depends which base they're coming from though. Could be an hour. It's probably on the other side of the African continent. Madagasca's got a big base."

Jeff checked his fuel gauges.

Leo noted this and did some calculations. "We have lots of fuel.. Don't worry about it. We can avoid more fighters and still have plenty of fuel to make it to Cairo."

"Does this bird have anything in the way of a threat detection system?" Jeff's eyes swept around the cockpit.

Leo laughed. "Come on, Jeff. This is a 747 not a B1. But let's monitor the radio. They might be stupid enough to transmit a message."

Gripen number 382

Abel was shocked when he heard the news: two Gripen Ds brought down by an unarmed Boeing 747. He almost didn't believe it when he was briefed. His mission was to go to the last known position of the 747, find it, and destroy it.

He thought about how the two Gripen pilots had failed. How had a 747 taken them down? Abel was nearly on top of the last known position of the 747 and turned on to the heading given by Gripen flight 12's Wingman.

I'm dead. He was one Gripen C, which was a much less advanced aircraft than the Gripen D and he was trying to do something that two Gripen Ds could not do.

He pulled his throttles back to eighty-six percent so he wouldn't miss seeing the 747 if he overflew it. He reached down and tuned his radio to one-one-decimal-nine so he could hear any transmission made by the 747 crew. He then turned on his infrared scanner and his nose radar and started his search.

"This is pointless," he muttered. "Even if I find this plane I'm not going to be able to down it if it really downed those two Gripen Ds." He realized that this was the second time he had told himself that. "If I keep thinking of that, then I'm most definitely dead." Abel glanced at his altimeter before returning his gaze to his small radar screen. He was a thousand feet above the water, a good height for a search. Then it hit him.

That thing has to have an armed escort. How else could it have downed the two Gripen Ds? He quickly armed his guns and all missiles then reset his radar and descended to five hundred feet. He monitored his radar closely, and glanced at his fuel gauge. He had 4,533 liters, or 2,000 kilometers worth of fuel left. That's when he spotted something on his radar. It was off his two o'clock. He hit the identify button. On his left-hand display screen the computer showed that it was a 747.

Africa Air flight 2367

Jeff checked his Tactical Collision Avoidance System display. He knew it would only display an aircraft if that aircraft's transponder was active. The display was blank. He ran a quick diagnostics. The results were good. The system was working. As soon as he returned his gaze to the TCAS monitor, it flickered on and off. The display began to move in a wave pattern and then disappeared altogether.

"We've lost the TCAS display,." Jeff said. He expected Leo to come over and make sure he had not made a mistake, but instead Leo did something that was totally out of character for him. He just hunched his shoulders and kept looking out the window.

"I'm not surprised," Leo said. "We've lost so much equipment I wouldn't be surprised if an engine falls off next."

Jeff laughed, not because they were in a funny situation. Being hunted by enemy fighters and not knowing where they were was a pilot's worst nightmare. No, he was laughing because earlier, when Leo was listing all the failures after the maneuver, he had thought the same thing.

Then Leo reached forward and started turning knobs.

"What are you doing?"

"Testing the autopilot. Last thing we need is for it to fail and for us to have to wrestle four hundred and fifty tons of crippled machine to Cairo."

Jeff looked out the window of the cockpit, and saw a small light off in the distance. *A fighter! But it's too low to be a fighter. It would be searching for them at a thousand feet. Must be a fishing boat.* "Hey, Leo. How's the fishing here?"

"The what?"

"The fishing." Jeff said, still looking at the small light.

"You did take a hit to the head when we did that maneuver. I'm going to go get you some oxygen." Leo reached down to unbuckle himself.

"I don't need oxygen. I'm serious. How's the fishing in this area?"

Leo reached for a chart behind him. "Not good. Why?"

"Look out there and tell me what you see."

Leo leaned forward so he could get a clear view of what his pilot was referring to. "It looks like a fishing vessel," Leo said after studying the small light in the distance.

"Yeah. That's what I thought, too, but... if, as you say, the fishing's no good here... What do you make of that light?"

Leo didn't respond. He was still looking out at the light outside the aircraft.

"Leo? What do—?"

Leo shot bolt upright in his seat. "It's a fighter!"

Gripen number 382

Abel could see a dot in the distance morph into the faint outline of a plane. He pushed his throttles to full afterburner and waited for the distance to close between the two planes. After a few seconds he could clearly see the 747 in the light of the moon. A small light flashed on his front display panel showing that the IRIS-T missiles were locked onto a target. He looked back at the 747 which had now turned away from his fighter.

No matter, he thought. His Gripen could easily outrun it. He was flying at nearly twice the speed of the 747 and was almost on top of it. He reached down, pulled the throttles back and deployed his spoilers to slow down. In response, the nose of the Gripen shot up and the airspeed began to bleed off. When he brought the nose back down and looked for the 747, it was gone. He had lost it.

Africa Air flight 2367

Jeff kept the 747 on its new heading as long as he could, but then he had to turn back on course to Cairo. He hoped that the turn had made the fast-moving fighter lose visual contact, but there was nothing he could do about what would happen once the fighter turned his radar back on. The 747 would show up as a huge dot on his radar screen and once that happened, the pilot could easily shoot it. Jeff reached down and pushed against the throttles to make sure they were at MAX.

"Anything we can do to lose him?" Jeff asked Leo as he stared out in front of the plane.

Leo, who was looking for the fighter out his cockpit window, sat back in his seat and grabbed the plane's maintenance guide.

That book won't help us. Jeff's mind returned to the explosives in the back of the plane. *How many boxes contain explosive?* he wondered.

"Nothing in here that can help us," Leo said, closing the Maintenance Manual.

"All right, take control. I'm going to see what we have that will go boom." Jeff got up from his seat and threw a radio to Leo. In the rear section, he checked each and every box. In the front passenger compartment, none of the boxes was marked EXPLOSIVE. He checked out a window for the fighter. He didn't see it, but he did see a plume of fire and smoke. He reached down and grabbed his radio.

"Leo! Missile! Bank left!"

The aircraft banked left immediately sending Jeff crashing into a box across the aisle. He could see the plume of smoke go past the window. He held onto the seat and waited for the missile to impact the right wing.

Gripen number 382

Abel watched in frustration as the missile passed off the right wing tip of the 747 automatically detonating after it missed the target. He cursed under his breath and then lined himself up for another shot. The 747 began flying in wide S turns, making it harder to take a shot, but not impossible. After a few seconds, Abel's Gripen was in position. He waited for the missile lock light to come on but it never illuminated. Abel reached down and ran a diagnostic. It came back positive.

"That's odd," Abel said. The 747 was now flying in a straight line instead of an S pattern. Suddenly the 747 started to climb and then it banked sharply to the left before leveling off a fair distance behind Abel's fighter. Abel brought his Gripen into a left turn in an attempt to follow the 747's movements. In response, the 747 began a turn and kept the distance between the two planes. Abel put his fighter into a climb and then pulled his throttles back to idle and let the 747 slip below him. He descended so he was right behind the 747, and then manually lined up a missile. The lock light didn't come on. He pushed the throttles forward and let the distance close a bit. Still no light. He brought the nose of the Gripen up a couple of degrees and launched a missile.

Africa Air flight 2367

"He's launched another missile!" Jeff yelled into his radio. "Break right!" The 747 immediately banked right, pressing Jeff against the window.

The missile flew off the left wingtip and passed the nose of the plane. It continued until it ran out of fuel and detonated harmlessly a few kilometers ahead of the 747.

"Missed," Leo breathed into his radio. "Missed."

"Yeah," said Jeff, "but don't get too excited. He still has missiles. And I'm sure he'd be happy to hit us with any one of them." He looked out the window again for the fighter. There was no sign of it.

Must be behind us getting ready. But then he saw him out of the corner of his window. It was performing S turns for no apparent reason. There was no armed aircraft near them... unless?

"He thinks we have an armed escort," Jeff said excitedly into his radio.

"Um...OK, but how does that help us exactly?"

"Make a radio transmission telling our supposed armed escort to approach."

"Good plan. Except for the fact that someone will hear us."

"No they won't. Use one-one-nine. The interceptors' channel." The fighter was now starting to fall behind the 747's tail.

"Then what?" Leo's response held uncertainty.

"It's like rushing in football. He'll think somebody's going to come shoot him down so he'll try to hit us as fast as possible. Hopefully he'll crack and mess up, waste his remaining missiles." Jeff was sure the plan would work.

"All right then, here goes nothin'."

Gripen number 382

"Escort one, we have a bogie on our tail and require assistance. We are passing waypoint Delta."

Abel was surprised. Even though he'd assumed they'd had an armed escort all along, it was odd hearing someone ordering your death. He yanked his Gripen C left and lined up perfectly behind the 747. He had to make this quick, before the escort got there. He lined up the missile manually and finally the missile lock light came on. He waited a few seconds to make sure. Then a missile passed over him. He watched as it screamed toward the 747. In an attempt to avoid it, the 747 began a bank right.

The escort! He yanked his fighter away.

"Gripen number 382 this is Gripen number 386. I'm here to help." Abel recognized the voice on his radio and the number given. It was his cousin, Keilfwe. Abel leveled off.

"Roger that. Fly at one hundred feet and come watch this 747 bite the dust." Abel turned to the 747 again.

"I'm right off your right wing tip by about a mile," Keilfwe stated.

"All right then, look out for an armed escort. They radioed for help a few minutes ago," Abel said, watching the 747 make a right turn. He looked ahead and saw that his cousin was right in its flight path.

Perfect! he thought. *Keilfwe can get him in the nose.* He leaned forward so he could get a good view of the explosion. What he saw made him cringe.

The 747 was flying lower than his cousin's plane but, as the 747 passed the other fighter, it started to climb. Keilfwe's missile tried to compensate and intercept the 747 but Keilfwe's plane was in the way. Abel watched as the missile plowed into his cousin's plane. All that was left were small pieces of flaming metal falling to the ocean below.

Hundreds of different things ran though Abel's mind. Did my cousin just kill himself? Man, this guy is good. I'm going to blow them out of the sky!

He turned his fighter to line up for another shot but found that the 747 was harder to aim at now. What was different? It was climbing and descending but he could easily match the movements. He had two missiles left.

"One at a time," he said to himself. "Even though it should only take one, save your missile just in case." His fighter was performing small jerks to each side. Abel looked down and saw that his hands were shaking so badly they were causing the plane to bank left and right. He could see the 747 trying to descend lower. He got behind it so he could aim properly.

Patrick Gloutney

On board the *MV Lamie*

Tambaso leaned back in his chair. It was a beautiful night, the stars were out and the moon provided light to illuminate the sea. He heard a bell. His fishing line! He ran over and grabbed the rod to reel in the fish. Then, he heard an ear splitting sound. Off in the distance, heading right for him, was a huge column of light and fire. He let go of his fishing rod which slipped below the surface of the water. A huge plane flew over his head and seconds later the missile that was trailing it hit the bridge of his vessel.

Africa Air flight 2367

"How many are there?" Leo screamed.

"I don't know! I only saw one and I thought he was hit with his own missile." Jeff saw a small flash of light out past the corner of his left rear cockpit window. "Oh no!"

"What? Don't tell me he's going to hit us." Leo leaned toward his window as much as his restraints would let him.

"It hit that fishing vessel we passed," Jeff said with concern in his voice. They had killed three fighter pilots and now an innocent fisherman. He pushed the 747 a bit lower. "How many missiles can a Gripen carry?" Jeff looked out over the nose of the aircraft, trying not to crash into the sea.

"About five. He shot us with two missiles that exploded off our wing tips. The third shot hit the other Gripen and then this guy just shot at us. So he could have three or four missiles left." Leo reached back into the knowledge he'd received as part of his training.

"No. The one we hit had four missiles under its wings. So this guy has only one missile left." Jeff was sure of it.

"Yeah, and a plane full of machine gun ammunition," Leo said.

Jeff's excitement quickly died off. Even if the fighter pilot missed with his last missile he would still be able to down the plane. Jeff glanced again at the fuel gauges. They were good. No leaks. No problems. He was about to tell Leo this bit of good news, when a flash of light erupted out of the left window as the last of the Gripen's missiles exploded after missing its target.

A piece of shrapnel crashed through the right side cockpit window and lodged itself into the floor next to Leo's foot. Leo let out a loud yell and reached down to make sure he had both his feet.

"OK?"

"Yes."

Jeff and Leo let out a synchronous sigh of relief.

"Good thing we were low this time," Leo said.

A laugh escaped from Jeff as he remembered the time he and Leo had once had a window shatter when they were at 30,000 feet. The force of that depressurization was such that if Jeff had not had his restraints on he would have gone flying out of the aircraft. That time, the cause had been poor maintenance. This time the window broke because of a missile.

"He is going to come up on our tail and shoot us with his guns," Jeff said. As if in response to his prediction, tracer bullets flew by his window.

"Good thing these guys are such lousy shots."

Gripen number 382

Abel was right on the tail of the 747. He was almost lined up for a good shot, with his guns pointed right below the tail fin. If he could hit there, he might be able to puncture an hydraulic line. The fluid would leak out causing the 747 to essentially bleed to death. Just as he was about to shoot, the 747 banked left.

"Why can't this guy stay still?" Abel put his Gripen C into a turn to follow the 747 but ended up flying over it. After he circled back he heard his computer say, "Bingo." This meant he had to turn back soon or he would not have enough fuel to get to a runway. But he was lined up perfectly to shoot the fuel tanks of the 747. If he hit the right spot, the fuel should leak onto the engine causing a fire, which should cause the 747 to explode. But again the 747 moved out of the way just in time. Cursing, Abel brought his fighter around to try again. This time he came head on to the 747, his guns pointed right at the cockpit window. Again, the 747 banked and got out of the way of the Gripen's guns.

"This guy is good," Abel muttered, "but I'm better." He brought his fighter around to line up again but the 747 had started a climb. Abel jammed the throttles forward and pointed his nose up so he could dive and shoot the 747 from above. They would not be expecting it. Then the unthinkable happened. Abel heard an alarm, and a yellow light—throbbing to show that he was low on fuel—turned red. In horror, he realized that when he had pointed his nose up, the fuel that was left had sloshed to the back of the tanks depriving his engine of fuel. He pushed his control stick forward but it was of no use. There was no power to move his control surfaces.

"You were a worthy adversary," he said to the crew of the 747 as his fighter fell to the ocean. He pulled the ejection handle between his legs. The fighter was too low and, while the canopy blew off like it was supposed to, the fighter slammed into the sea before Abel's seat fired out of the cockpit. Trapped in his seat he was dragged to the bottom of the ocean.

Africa Air flight 2367

"OK, that one is down," Leo said in relief.

The fuel gauges told Jeff they had just enough fuel to make it to Cairo. "How are you doing with that broken window?" he asked.

"A bit drafty but I'll survive."

Once Jeff was sure that there were no more fighters, he activated the auto pilot and eased back into his seat. "Who says a 747 is no fun to fly?"

The men laughed.

"It is a tad different from our small fighters, though. Wouldn't you say?"

Jeff thought back to when they had received their briefing. He thought it was crazy to think that a 747 could beat a Gripen. But here he was now, after avoiding and destroying four Gripens—and one unfortunate fishing vessel.

"How long until we reach Cairo?"

Leo did some calculations and looked at his watch. "About forty-nine minutes to go."

"How is that possible?"

"We're going pretty fast, Jeff." Leo pointed at the water rushing by.

Cairo, 0210 h

When Aly arrived at the airfield, his eyes swept along the line-up of people ready for a briefing.

"Good morning, everyone. I'm sorry for the hour, but we must be ready. In five minutes, a 747 will land. This plane must be unloaded and hidden in a hangar by sunrise. The aircraft may be damaged and that's why we have the heavy machinery here. If the aircraft can't move under its own power, it will be pulled or pushed to the hangar. Understood?"

Every person at the airfield said the same thing, "Yes, sir."

Aly looked around once again and then continued, "Good, then get into positions. We have three minutes." He watched as everyone rushed to comply.

"Sir, what if the plane doesn't make it?" Aband asked.

"We will wait until 0400," said Aly, his voice full of concern. "If it doesn't show, we will assume that it was downed, and leave." He couldn't afford to wait any longer. The FAR was successful because they never stayed in one place for too long. If there was even a hint of trouble, they were gone. This shipment not arriving would most likely cause them to vacate the area for at least three years. If not more. The boss was very strict about this. Aly had heard stories about people messing up and who had been called to see the boss, never to return.

Africa Air flight 2367

"Let's start the landing checklist," Jeff said. He brought the 747 to a thousand feet. As they went through the checklist, Jeff kept an eye out for any fighters that might have trailed them to Cairo.

"OK, that's it. All we need to do is put the gear down," Leo said as he put the checklist back into its pocket.

"Put it down now. We don't want to have to go around because of the gear not working."

Leo reached forward and moved the gear lever to the down position and all four gear status indicators showed up green.

Jeff let out a sigh of relief and lined the nose up with the heading where the runway was supposed to be and waited for it to come into view. "Runway twelve o'clock," he called out and began to descend.

"I'll put the flaps down but we don't know how fast we're going," Leo said. He reached down and pulled the flaps lever down one notch. Nothing. He pulled them down another notch. Again, nothing happened. When he put them down one more notch, an alarm rang and the sound of tearing metal ripped through the aircraft as the flaps flew off.

"Flap over speed!" Leo yelled.

"We need to put this thing down now." Jeff exclaimed. As if in response, there was a tremendous tearing noise as all of the gear doors ripped off. They were less than fifteen seconds from touchdown. Jeff began to flare the nose of the 747 gently to ensure that they did not break any of the damaged parts of the 747. The aircraft slowly approached the runway.

"It has been a pleasure serving with you, Leo," was last thing said between the two pilots before the landing gear touched the ground. The main gear held but the nose gear hit the ground hard enough to break it off. The 747 went skidding off the runway, plowing into three parked cars, and then continued toward the main building. Jeff hit his head on the main instrument panel and was thrown against his chair. He was momentarily knocked unconscious.

He came to with a splitting headache. He reached up to wipe moisture from his forehead. When he brought his hand down it was covered in blood. He looked over to see that Leo was unconscious and bleeding from a huge gash in his arm. Jeff could hear voices outside. He reached back, grabbed the fire ax and smashed out the window. He looked down and saw that he was also bleeding, from his shoulder. Before he could do anything else, the cockpit door swung open and Aband rushed in with the medics. Jeff tried to wave, but fell unconscious.

Cairo Hospital

Jeff woke up to Aband standing over him. "Did we do it?" he asked weakly.

"Yeah, you guys did it."

As Aband spoke, a smile spread across each of their faces but Jeff felt his smile disappear quickly. "Did Leo make it?"

"You aren't going to get rid of me that easy." Leo hobbled into the room on crutches. The smile quickly returned to Jeff's face. Leo's arm was bandaged.

"Why the crutches?" Jeff asked as he tried to sit up, but Aband gently pushed him back down, shaking his head.

"Nothing serious." Leo gestured to his foot. "The shrapnel that flew through the window cut my leg up pretty bad so I have to stay off it for a few weeks. That's all."

"You, on the other hand, were messed up pretty bad," Aband said. Then pointing out every injury as he spoke, he continued. "You had a big cut on your forehead. Possible concussion from that. You passed out. Do you remember that? Your shoulder's messed up. You had a minor cut to your leg... Oh, and you hurt your lower back as well so they don't want you to sit up yet."

The smile faded from Jeff's face as he thought about his career. "Will I be able fly again?" He was trying to move his toes and found that he could.

He then tried moving other parts of his body.

"Will you be able to fly?" Aband said this with humor in his voice. "After this mission FAR will do anything to keep you in the air."

The smile returned to Jeff's face. He could keep flying, and more importantly, he had lived to tell the tale of the recent flight.

"That reminds me. The FAR will let you two fly any plane you want and they're going to promote both of you up two ranks."

Jeff looked at Leo and they both nodded.

"I think we'll keep flying our fighters and the 747s, Aband," Jeff said. "But don't ever put us on one of those crazy supply missions again."

"Don't worry. The FAR appreciates what you guys did but there's no need for the project now that we have the weapons. They are working on a safer way to get supplies." Aband's grin was wide. "Now... How about when you guys get out of the hospital, I buy you a beer."

"Sounds good to me. How about you, Jeff?" Leo asked and then reached up and flattened out his hair.

"Yeah. I could really go for a beer."

Cairo

"The mission was completed successfully," Aly said.

"Were there casualties?" Fredrick Hurley asked.

Aly sighed. Fredrick Hurley was Secretary of Defense of the United States of America and he always expected casualties. Although he wanted the reports he never thought of the casualties as being actual men. He simply thought of them as numbers and power lost.

"Not to us, but the 747 was damaged beyond repair. Only a small percent of supplies were dam—"

"How much?"

"About five percent. The aircraft was heavily damaged but thanks to the design, the cabin and cargo hold remained largely intact, protecting the majority of the weapons." Aly paused to gauge Hurley's reaction. "Unfortunately the pilots were hurt but are recovering well. The lighter weapons are en route to the storage area. The heavier artery is awaiting transport." Aly sat back down in his seat. "This concludes my report."

"Thank you, Aly." The head of the Free Army Republic's voice came from a set of speakers at the far end of the table. No one had ever met the man and none of the men in the room even knew his name. The Free Army Republic had been this man's creation. He had assembled the best mercenaries into an army that had only one objective. Money.

"Anything else to report?"

"Yes, sir," General Dalton Murree said.

Aly often thought of Fredrick Hurley's younger step-brother as the exponential of his brother. He was younger and smaller and just behind his brother in the US military chain of command.

"I did some calculations and, based on the amount of weapons we have and the estimated strength of the island military—" Murree began.

"How do we know the strength of the military?" Aly asked.

"We have two contacts inside the island military, turned while they were attending college," the head of FAR stated. "Go on, Dalton."

"We have an eighteen percent chance of capturing the island." Shouts of displeasure went up around the table.

"Have you rechecked this data?" Hurley asked.

"I have gone over the results multiple times," Murree said.

"So I put two men through the worst moments of their lives for nothing?" Aly spat.

"No," Murree said. "I believe we can use the damaged aircraft to our advantage. The United States' definition of national security is fairly loose. If my brother were to get us a meeting with the President then we could bring forward information on how this island had caused the crash of an unarmed civilian airliner. Couldn't we?" Murree raised his eyebrows in a question.

"That's—" Aly said.

"Not now, Aly. I think Fredrick... er... Dalton is onto something."

"Yeah. We could easily falsify some reports," one of the men suggested.

"What about something a little different?" Everyone stared at Aly. "If we create this information, then the whole thing will probably get to the press."

Some of those present nodded but Murree looked enraged.

Aly continued. "The fact is that the island is supplying fuel for shipping vessels. What's stopping them from modifying the fuel so that it works for automobiles? Before you know it, the oil industry in the US will die and that, combined with their huge debt, could possibly cause their economy to collapse. With no economy, they can't fund their oversized military and *then* you have a threat to national security." There was a long moment of silence after his proposal.

"How will this benefit us? If the US captures the island, they'll keep it for themselves and then we *will* be left with nothing." Aly looked around the room to gauge reactions.

Fredrick Hurley spoke up. "The US will take it for themselves—no doubt about that—but we can still make a lot of money. The US will need to contract the management of the island's resources out to a private company. If the Free Army Republic were to form a shell company, I'm in a position to secure the contract for that company. Then, because the island would be top secret, it would be easy to siphon money to the FAR without causing suspicion."

"You're right," the disembodied voice at the head of table said. "If that doesn't work, then we will use the 747 as back-up. General?"

"Sir," both brothers answered.

"Fredrick," the voice said. "You are to present this to the President of the United States. Make it happen!"

White House, Oval Office

"You want me to what?" the President asked incredulously after Fredrick Hurley had proposed his idea.

"A small group of individuals have brought forward information on an island that could pose a threat to our national security. I propose that we launch an attack on them before it can happen," Hurley explained.

"So you want me to launch an unprovoked attack on this little island because they make gas?" The President asked, puzzled.

"Essentially, yes," Hurley responded.

"You've lost it. How can a little island be a threat to our national security?"

"You see..." Hurley reiterated Aly's reasoning to the President.

"Never thought of it that way," the President said. "But it's still crazy. If the thing goes south it might ruin the country—and me."

"That's the beauty of it," Hurley pressed. "The fact that the people who live on the island keep themselves hidden from the rest of the world will make it impossible for anyone to know about the attack. Once we capture the island, we take over all their trading agreements. Our country will profit greatly. Maybe even enough to get us out of debt."

"Humph. Interesting theory," the President said.

Hurley knew he had the man now. "Imagine. You would be remembered as the President who pulled this great country out of debt."

Hurley knew the President would love to be remembered as such. He was now confident that he wouldn't need the damaged 747.

"You're right. It could be a threat. Calculate how many aircraft, boats and men you'll need and then double it. I don't want any chance of failure. Understood?" The President looked at him over top of his glasses. A slight smile tugged at one corner of his mouth.

"Perfectly, sir." Hurley saluted, turned on his heel and left the Oval Office.

Too easy.

On board the gunship *Magenta*, lead ship of the Serenidad marine command

"One inbound!" the radar operator shouted out. "High. At 28,000 feet. Four-engine, 707 reconnaissance aircraft."

"I think they found us," Chris said. Chris was the captain of the *Magenta,* a state-of-the-art gunship. She was completely streamlined to save energy and was painted dark blue, grey, black, and white to disguise her. Chris was also the commander of the Serenidad's Navy protecting the island and its people from anyone one who was ignorant enough to try to take the island by force.

They were thirty kilometers offshore of the little island in the Pacific Ocean. The ship was rocking in the waves of a blistering storm. Rain pelted the clear roof of the Bridge so hard that Chris imagined it might come crashing in on him.

"Multiple inbounds from west! Low. Less than 1000 feet. They're A-10s."

Chris turned around and hit a red BATTLE STATIONS button. A loud alarm sounded throughout the ship and men rushed to various points on the ship. He looked out to see one of the two anti-air/anti-ship guns swivel up so they were pointed at the sky in front of the ship.

And so it begins, Chris thought. "Alert HQ about our findings and alert the battle groups at the west end of the patrols. Weapons, if they're armed and come in range, knock 'em dead."

"*Cheetah* battle group reports under attack by anti-ship missiles," the radar operator shouted. "New inbound from the west. Low and fast. It's an F16. *Cheetah* reports the minesweeper *Hawk* is damaged and taking on water. *Cheetah*'s been hit. They're evacuating the *Hawk*. *Cheetah* reports the frigate *Trans* is going under. More inbounds from the north. South. East. They're everywhere!"

Just then, the *Magenta's* guns ripped into the night sky and a huge fireball that was an A-10, erupted in front of the *Magenta* and crashed into the water beside her. The port gun swung outward and downed another A-10.

"*Cheetah* reports that its whole battle group is damaged. They're evacuating all four ships." the radar operator shouted.

"Have the *Gate* battle group help with the rescue and protect them." The display screen off to Chris's left displayed all the names of the ships he had under his control and slowly red lines were appearing everywhere, indicating that a ship was either destroyed or too crippled to fight.

Radar continued to report: "The *Jets* battle group reports they have downed one A-10 and more are coming. They report losing one ship. They've been hit!"

Chris felt his heart skip a beat. The *Jets* battle group was one of the most advanced battle groups and they could not stop a bunch of A-10 warthogs?

This brought a grim thought to Chris's mind. *We may not be able to hold them off.*

"Radio for aerial assistance. I want every ship covered."

A set of lights snapped on. Chris turned and closed his eyes to avoid being flash-blinded. Chris could hear bullets raking across the *Magenta*'s hull. He looked out behind the ship as an F16 sped off into the distance.

"Radar, I want warnings before those aircraft get close. Got it?"

Chris turned his attention to the guns. They were shooting at a low-flying missile which immediately exploded. Another aircraft exploded out in front. The screen that displayed all the ship names was showing more and more red lines every second.

Sir. Missile launch." someone called out.

"Dive! Dive! Dive!"

On board USA F16 number 345 *Reaper*

A perfect missile launch, Jessie thought as the missile sped straight for the ship in front of her. The ship began a turn to avoid the missile. Its bow dipped into a wave and the vessel disappeared under the water. The missile exploded harmlessly above the water.

Odd, Jessie puzzled. As she pushed her aircraft into a turn, another ship soon came into view. She pressed the missile launch button and watched as this missile plowed into the side of the ship which instantly listed. She came back to finish it off with one of her two remaining missiles and found it on its side.

"F16 number 345. Another ship down. There was something odd though. I fired at one and it behaved almost like a submarine. It slipped below the waves before the missile impacted."

"Roger, 345," a voice said, uncertain.

He doesn't believe me.

"You are near bingo. Turn heading 270 for refueling," the voice ordered.

Shaking her head, Jessie banked her aircraft sharply but as she headed back for the tanker, a ship appeared out of the water and started firing. Although she yanked her fighter away, it wasn't soon enough. Warning lights flashed and alarms sounded. Jessie assessed her situation: her only engine's RPMs were dropping fast. She was low, not going too fast and she had a gunship on her tail. Not good. She positioned her fighter so it was going in the direction of the waves. That way it would have the best chance of surviving. She grabbed the ejection handles between her legs, did one last check and pulled as hard as she could. Instantly the canopy blew off the fighter and she was projected out like a rocket.

The events that followed were a blur but eventually she found herself being lifted onto the deck of a ship. Her eyes focused on the men standing above her. She was then pulled to her feet and half pushed, half dragged below decks into what appeared to be the hall of some sort of a jail. A man waiting there put a needle into her arm. Then they threw her into a dark room. She grabbed one man and pulled him close to her. As they closed the door shut she punched him in the gut. He retaliated by throwing her to the cell floor and drawing his weapon.

Drowsiness hit her and she fell unconscious.

On board the Serenidad Navy destroyer *Rose*

Cynthia looked to the front of the Bridge. Her whole battle group was burning except for her ship and the frigate *Village Bound*. She rushed to the radar screen on the left of the Bridge where she saw that the fighters were attacking ships and not heading inland.

"Order *Village Bound* to come alongside. I want the engines left running and everybody off this boat." In response, everyone rushed to the transfer station. "Tell the *Village Bound* that after we're onboard they are to pick up survivors from the other ships."

"Ma'am?" Brad, commander of the weapons crew, addressed her. "Why are we evacuating? The ship's barely damaged."

"I'm going to drive it away from the battle group and draw the fighters' attention away from the damaged ships."

"You are not doing this alone," Clyde shouted. "Can't possibly man all the stations alone!"

"You need someone to report our position."

"You need to make sure your engines stay running."

"And you need weapons if you plan on succeeding."

"So you all want to risk your lives to save this battle group?"

All four crewmembers nodded.

"Okay, Radio Chris about what we're doing. Get the weapons and any crew willing to man them ready. Make sure you make it clear that this is voluntary. Same for you, Engineering. Helm, make sure we don't hit *Village Bound.*" Cynthia sat and pressed the intercom button. "I want anyone not spoken to off this boat in ten minutes!"

"Ma'am..."

"Can the ma'am stuff. You know my name is Cynthia."

"Sorry. I informed the Navy commander and he doesn't like the idea at all."

Cynthia laughed, shaking her head. Off duty I'm Chris's sister, but on duty I'm the commander of a battle group. He'll just have to deal with it. "Tough."

The time seemed to drag on as she waited for the crew to evacuate the ship. *Finally!* "Clyde. Pull ahead and get distance between the other ships." Soon the light of the burning ships looked like nothing but a pocket lamp. "Okay light 'er up like a Christmas tree."

Clyde threw various switches and all the exterior lights snapped on. Thane moved over to the radar station beside him and turned all the radar that were on STANDBY to TRANSMIT. Sure enough, the fighters went for the obvious target leaving the damaged ship to sink.

"They're coming!" Thane shouted.

The sound of missiles launching filled the air as two of the ship-to-air missiles on the *Rose* launched skyward. Flashes of light appeared as they hit their targets.

"Three aircraft, low, less than ten kilometers!" A missile plowed into the upper portion of the stern of the ship. Another hit her mid-section. The deck sagged but she stayed afloat. The guns ripped into the night sky and more missiles were launched.

Cynthia spotted a missile heading right for the Bridge. "Hit the dirt!" She yelled, throwing herself to the floor.

The missile malfunctioned. It tore through the Bridge but didn't explode. Cynthia stood to find there was no one else alive on the Bridge. They were either nowhere to be seen or were spread in pieces across the Bridge. She gagged at the sight and lurched forward, stepping on the mutilated body of Thane. She screamed and began to cry. Then the mid-section of the vessel gave way. It sank in just under two minutes taking her and the rest of her crew with it.

On board the gunship *Magenta*

"Sir, the *Rose* reports that it is heavily damaged and... Sorry, sir. We've lost contact with the *Rose*."

Chris sat back in his seat. "No. No, no," he said softly. The *Magenta's* guns ripped into the sky once again causing another fireball.

"Sir, four A-10s low coming from all directions." Both guns began a sawing motion back and forth, lighting up the sky with tracers and knocking down two of the A-10s. Then the port side gun abruptly stopped. "Sir, Weapons reports the port gun is jammed."

Chris was about to respond when the sound of jet engines rang through the ship. The two surviving A-10s came in, raking the ship with machine-gun fire. Smoke filled the Bridge and the deck pitched to the left.

"*Sir.* Engineering reports they have lost control of the port ballast system."

The ship shuddered and rolled onto her side. "Dive! Dive! Dive!" Chris yelled. "Bottom her until we can get the ballast system fixed." The ship slipped below the water and started to level out. "Put her down gen—"

The *Magenta* slammed onto the ocean floor. The impact knocked him down and smashing his head into a rail. The ship slid along the ocean floor for the next four kilometers before hitting an underwater boulder and abruptly stopping.

Chris grabbed hold of the seat next to him and lifted himself off the floor. He looked around the Bridge. Most of the display screens had cracked or ruptured altogether. He walked from station to station checking the injured, some of whom were already receiving medical attention. He reached the helmsman who was pinned beneath a fallen control panel.

"Sir, your head. It's cut."

Chris looked at his reflection in one of the cracked display screens. He was bleeding but it was obvious that it was not serious. "Don't worry about me. Right now we're going to get this thing off your leg." He motioned for one of the crewmen. The crewman pointed to Chris's head but he waved him off. "Help me get this off Ian's leg." They handed Ian to the medic crew.

"Sir, Engineering says they can fix the ballast system but we might be here a while. The ship hit the ground hard and damaged the props."

Chris shook his head. "So we're out of the battle. All right, tell them to do their best. Make sure they know that the life support system takes priority." Chris moved to the edge of the Bridge and made out the faint outline of another ship sinking through the water. "I hope the rest of the fleet can hold them off."

After a couple hours of making rounds and inspecting each station, Chris was finally on his way down to the brig.

"Who do we have down here?" Chris asked the guard. The guard handed a sparse dossier to him and responded smiling.

"It's Jessie Jones. We think she's Tom and Betty's daughter."

"The Joneses' daughter? Interesting." Chris walked down to cell 3 and opened the door. The woman inside took a swing at him right away. He blocked it and slammed the door behind him before any guard could enter. The woman tried to kick him but he grabbed her leg and flipped her onto the floor. She jumped up and continued the fight. She got a few good hits in on Chris, but he was able to block most of them. He hit the woman in the side, knocking her down, put his foot on her chest, pulled a knife out of his boot, then removed his foot and knelt down so his face was inches from hers.

"You are a good fighter, I'll give you that. What are your people planning?"

There was no reply.

"Look, if you aren't going to talk..." He placed the back side of the blade to her throat, "... you are no use to me. I might as well dispose of you now. It's your choice." He could tell she was weighing her options.

"You wouldn't kill me," she grunted.

"Don't be so sure. Your people killed my sister. You sank my Navy's ships and killed my men. You, yourself probably logged four... five kills."

"Seven, actually. I got seven of your ships." She laughed. "It was easy."

"Yeah? Well we got most of your aircraft."

"No you didn't. If you did then what was...? Wait. You're the ship I shot at? The one that disappeared under the water before the missile hit you?" Her pupils widened. "You're the one who shot me down."

"That we are. And we're currently preparing this ship for another patrol. So we'll soon be back up there to make sure none of your friends gets away. Unless you help me, you can join them in the sea depths." He pressed harder on the knife.

"I'd rather die than help you," Jessie said, spitting in Chris's face.

"Suit yourself." Chris stood up. "It's Jessie, right?"

There was no response from the pilot. She was looking around the room almost as if she were planning her escape.

"Your father helped build this ship," Chris said and then turned to leave.

"My father...? My parents live in Florida."

"They moved here a few years ago. The founder of the island's son took a liking to your dad's mechanical skills. He was actually the one who made this ship possible."

Jessie tried to move but Chris put his foot back on her chest.

"Don't you see? Your own people tried to kill your parents. Just like they did my sister."

A tear ran down the side of Jessie's face. "No, no, no. You're lying."

"They don't care who they hurt, just as long as they get what they want. We stand to protect this island and the lifestyle it permits," he shouted in her face.

A few seconds of silence ensued before Jessie responded. "My parents' mailing address is still Florida. I sent them a package last week. They always write back."

"We divert their mail. No one in the US knows they live here," Chris said.

"I'll help you for now but rest assured that I'm only doing it to keep my parents safe. If you're lying, you'll regret it."

Chris removed his foot from her chest.

With a heavy sigh Jessie struggled to sit up. "This was just the first part. We did this to weaken your defenses. The final blow will come in two weeks, when we land thousands of marines on your island and take over."

"Why the two-week delay?"

"Give you a chance to surrender. I hope you'll do for my parents' sake."

"Thanks." Chris turned and left. "She'll help us," he said to the guards, putting his knife away. "Make sure she's comfortable." He walked through the hall to the elevator which he took down to Engineering.

"How long until we can get back to the island?" he asked as he walked in.

"We'll be moving by morning," someone snarled. "No sooner so don't—"

"Don't use that tone with the captain!" the head engineer, Paul, shouted. "Sorry about that, Chris. He's a little stressed right now."

"We all are. How did your section fare after impact?"

"We did OK. A few bumps and bruises but we'll survive. We have divers working on the props as we speak. Like the lad said, we'll be moving by morning."

Chris nodded.

"You OK? I heard about Cynthia."

Chris stopped in his tracks, feeling sadness claw at him. It had been the first time he had actually had a chance to think of his sister. He fought back the tears that welled in his eyes. "Bad news travels fast," was all Chris said before leaving.

On board the Serenidad Navy frigate *Perl*

"Sir, there are reports that *Magenta* has been sunk."

"What?" Captain Dave shouted.

"A destroyer in the area said an A-10 got some gunshot off at the *Magenta* and she was on her side. It's unknown if she recovered by diving but there are no reports of seeing her."

Dave sat down, shocked.

"All right. Make sure—"

"F-111's. Low. Looks like a couple flights," a radar operator informed him.

"Put us in their flight path and nail 'em," Dave shouted. The ship started a slight turn before abruptly stopping. The deceleration was so violent that Dave almost fell onto the deck.

"We've run aground, sir."

"That's impossible! What ground is there out here?"

"Wait, sir. Depth below keel is increasing. Sonar reports it's a sub. We've hit a sub! Front Weapons reports we're taking on water. Sonar reports the sub still dropping."

"Drop depth charges. I want that sub dead."

The deck had begun to list forward. They might not be able to fight much longer.

"Sonar reports sub has hit the floor. I repeat, sub has hit the floor."

Patrick Gloutney

An A-10 flew overhead, cannons blaring, followed by three F-111s.

Why are they using A-10s? Dave wondered.

"Engineering reports forward flood control system has failed. They recommend evacuation, sir. They say we have five minutes before mandatory."

"We fight as long as we can. Regardless. Inform HQ about the sub. Sonar, I want a count of how many subs there are." Dave slammed his fist on his arm rest. "HQ must be supplied with that information, too," he added angrily.

"Sonar reports there's only the one that hit the floor. At the moment. Three A-10s. One low, two high. The top two are diving on us."

"Helm, can we move?" Dave shouted.

The helmsmen shook his head.

"Notify HQ about this tactic they are using."

A missile plowed into the bow of the *Perl* and machine gun bullets pelted her from above and starboard.

Dave hit the EVACUATE alarm button but it was too late, the ship sank before Dave and most of the crew could react.

On board the Serenidad Navy patrol boat *Tracker*

Zac watched from his gun turret as yet another A-10 swooped in on their ship. None of them had fired a shot yet, almost like they were teasing them, flying too close for the missiles but too fast for the guns. Nevertheless, Zac tried to hit them as they flew over. He got lucky with the next fighter. The bullets ripped through one of the missiles on its wing. The explosion was magnificent but there was a price to pay. The next A-10 raked the side of the vessel with its cannons. The bullets caused a gun turret at the bow to jam, and then the next fighter jammed Zac's gun and caused an explosion at the stern. He looked over to see a crewman without an arm crawling across the deck.

What's he doing? Zac grabbed his machine gun and ran out of the safety of his turret. He threw himself to the deck as another fighter passed overhead. He could hear missiles hitting other boats in the battle group. He crawled over to the injured crewman.

"Get below decks" he yelled and rolled onto his back, firing his machine gun at a passing A-10.

"My arm. It hurts... The pain's too much," the crewmen grunted. He withdrew a .45 caliber pistol from his holster and placed the muzzle against his right temple.

"No!" Zac grabbed the injured man's arm and pulled the gun away from his head. The crewman pulled the trigger and the bullet tore through

Zac's right shoulder. The injured crewman looked at Zac in horror. Zac felt no pain in his shoulder. He stood and lifted the man up with his good arm, opened a door and pushed him below decks. A missile plowed into the side of the ship. Zac was knocked off his feet as the ship violently jolted sideways. He felt a stab of shearing pain in his leg. He looked down to learn that his lower left leg was missing. A flash of light erupted out over the water and in the light Zac could see a B52. He grabbed his radio off his belt but never had a chance to report the bomber. Its missile hit the ship, instantly destroying most of the lower sections and rolling what was left onto its side. Zac fell into the ocean just before a second missile plowed into the dying ship. The explosion obliterated Zac and all that was left of the *Tracker*.

On board the *Magenta*

Sitting on his bed, Chris glanced at the clock on the stand. It was 0100. Unlike most of the crew—except for Engineering—he had not been able to sleep. His mind kept flashing images of Cynthia, images of the *Rose* burning with Cynthia lying dead on its deck. His mind searched every possible way it could to come up with how his sister's ship could have been destroyed. He got up and dressed. He walked down to Engineering and into a room crowded with all the Engineering crew. He stood there waiting for the crowd to clear, but when it didn't, he tapped an engineer in front of him on the shoulder. The man jumped and looked at Chris in surprise.

"What's going on?"

"They were testing the ballast system when a fire started," the man said patting down his grease-covered clothing.

Chris was shocked.

The engineer obviously saw this and started laughing. "Don't worry, it's out now. It was a garbage fire caused by a foolish man throwing a live cigarette into the can."

Chris breathed a sigh of relief.

"So now we are all being searched for cigarettes. The chief's up there if you want him."

Chris nodded his thanks and moved to the front of the room. "Hey, Chief, is everybody all right?"

"Oh yeah just a—"

"Garbage fire started by a cigarette. I know."

The chief looked at his good friend with a puzzled expression. "You know what? I give up trying to find out how you learn these things."

"I have my ways." The two men laughed. "I know safety's first... but... When you find who's responsible for this, let me know will ya?" The chief nodded and Chris left for the elevator.

"Chris. Wait. Here." The chief tossed Chris a clipboard. "It's our progress. Thought you might like to know."

"You know me too well," Chris said with a grin. He moved out of the room and made his way to the elevator. Once on the dark Bridge, he turned the light on and sat in his chair. He thought he saw something moving out in the water so he turned the light off and saw a huge black sausage-like object through the Bridge window. He hit the red BATTLE STATIONS button and seconds later a launch tube arose from the *Magenta*'s deck and the Bridge crew rushed in, most of them out of uniform.

"There's a sub out there," he said. "Which means things are getting worse for the rest of our Navy. I want anything that passes by that is not our own, dead. Understood?"

The group responded by heading to their stations.

Before Chris could say another word, a torpedo shot out of the tube and hit the sub floating in front of them. Smaller explosions erupted around the sub. From what Chris could tell, they were depth charges, which meant that one of their own ships was also attacking the sub. Chris smiled and looked up as another torpedo passed over the Bridge. When the water settled, a bright light appeared off to his right. His smile quickly vanished.

"Hit the lights," he said, afraid of what he might see.

The lights snapped on illuminating the sub they had attacked lying on the sea floor with two huge holes in its hull. But it also illuminated a war ship—or what was left of one. It was in pieces, the biggest pieces twisting until they broke.

"Get a picture of its bow. I want to know what ship that is."

In a moment the radar operator brought a portable display screen to Chris.

Chris sat back in his seat, dragged a heavy hand down across his face and sighed. "It's the *Village Bound.* The last remaining ship from the *Rose* battle group. It had all the survivors on board." Chris slammed his fist onto the armrest of his chair and pressed angrily onto the intercom button. "How long until we can get back in the fight?"

"Sorry, Chris, but like I said we shan't be moving until morning. And the port gun's still jammed so it will be pretty hard to fight."

"It is morning," Chris growled.

"What? Oh. Well, by morning I meant around sunrise. Somewhere between 0600 and 0700, I'd say."

Chris clicked off the line. I hate this. We're stuck here and our fleet is being pounded.

White House Situation Room

"OK. What's the status on this mission I let you talk me into," the President of the United States asked his Secretary of Defense, Fredrick Hurley.

"Sir, the mission was a complete success. We shot down most of the Air Force and we decimated their Navy. In fact, there were no ships left in the end according to our crews." Hurley's assistant handed him a bundle of papers. Hurley glanced at them and frowned and his throat went dry.

"I take it those are the casualty reports?" the President sighed.

Hurley nodded.

"Well then, let's hear it. How many did we lose?"

Hurley did not reply. He was staring at the list of causalities.

"Well, Mr. Secretary?"

"N...N...No one made it back," he whispered, dumbfounded.

"Speak up. We don't have all day." The President folded his hands in front of him, obviously losing his patience.

"No one made it back, sir. But keep in mind that the mission was a complete success." Hurley handed the papers to the shocked President, while the rest of the room went silent in disbelief.

"What? All the A-10s, F16s, F-111s, B52s? The subs? How did this happen?"

Hurley shook his head. "We don't know, sir. They were much tougher than we thought. But that doesn't matter because they now can't defend themselves—"

"It doesn't matter?" the President snapped, slamming his fist on his polished oak desk. "We've lost hundreds of good men and women."

Everyone in the room started to add their own opinions loudly. "Sir, you cannot think to proceed with this mission." The General Secretary yelled more loudly than the rest.

"*Quiet.* All of you. This mission must go on," said Hurley.

The room fell silent.

"No, Hurley," the President said angrily. "He's right. How do you expect me to authorize another strike when the first team didn't make it back?"

"But sir. We are so close to victory. We could send a second strike package right away and have the island in a couple of hours." Hurley tapped the bundle of papers in his hand. "I have it all arranged. All you have to do is say the word."

"What? You organized a strike package without authorization? I'll bet the bases are even on alert. Are they?"

Hurley nodded. "Sir, I did this in the best interest of our—"

"You did this in your own interests! No one else's."

"That doesn't matter. What matters is we get the island. It's valuable both economically and defensively."

"And what if you're wrong and this island turns out to be useless?" the President demanded.

"It *is* valuable," Hurley snapped then quickly moderated his tone. "Remember the threat this island possesses." When he received no reply, he continued. "Sir, we must avenge those who died. By calling off the strike, you make their sacrifices meaningless. How do you explain that to the families? They died so the US could get that island. Honor them by getting what they were fighting for. We can do that in hours."

The President was silent for a moment.

"Fine, we continue. But you are to follow the plan. I will try to make contact and get them to surrender before we strike in the next few weeks. Understood?"

"Yes, sir!" Hurley said happily.

The President waved his hand to dismiss the meeting and Hurley hurried out of the White House, his aide close behind him. They climbed into a waiting limo.

"Why the hurry, sir?" his aide panted.

"We need to get back to the base fast." Hurley looked out the window of the limo. "I want the strike forces ready as soon as possible. I'm going to try to talk to the President tomorrow. I want to shorten the lag between attacks."

On board the gun ship *Magenta*

The *Magenta* lurched to the side, knocking Chris off his feet. He barely missed hitting the now-blood-stained rail in front of him. After regaining his footing, Chris looked outside. They were still on the ocean floor. He pressed his intercom button.

"Engineering. What happened?"

"Sorry about that, Chris. We were testing the ballast system and one of the newbies got excited."

"Do the best you can." Chris glanced at his watch. It was 0546. He had now been awake for a full thirty-two hours, yet he didn't feel tired. He looked around at the Bridge crew. Some were manning their stations normally and some were cleaning up and repairing equipment. The low rumble of the engines could be heard and the ship lurched upward. Chris pressed the intercom button again. "Hey, Chief. It's not 0600 yet," he joked.

"Yeah. We jumped the gun. If you want, I can put her back down."

Chris laughed. "Don't you dare. I ain't no burbot." The whole Bridge crew chuckled at the reference to the bottom-dwelling fish they were often compared to. "How long can we stay submerged, Chief?"

"As long as we need to. But it might be better to stay on the surface," came the reply.

"All right then. Ian, head back to base so we can fix that gun but don't keep us submerged. I want any trigger-happy American we see, dead."

The Hidden Island

The *Magenta* broke the water's surface in just a few seconds and what Chris saw made his gut turn over. The water running down the sides of the clear cover over the Bridge was black. Fires were burning on the water and every wave they hit sent more black water onto the ship.

"Unbelievable," he muttered to himself. "Radio—"

"Sir! Mines! All around us! They aren't ours!" someone shouted.

"Full stop."

The low rumble of the engines changed to a roar and the boat slowed to a halt. "Sonar, I want a picture of the mine layout. Updated every thirty seconds."

Soon a sailor handed a portable display screen to Chris. "They're all tethered, sir."

Chris nodded. "Get one to Ian as well."

The mines were everywhere. He studied the image before calling out. "Port ten degrees. Make speed 8 knots." A few seconds passed. "Starboard 20 degrees." Chris continued to direct the ship until they were clear of the mine field, which ended just twelve nautical miles off the shore of the island. "Ian. I want you to memorize this mine field so you can navigate it as fast as possible."

The helmsmen nodded in agreement.

They pulled into the harbor entrance. It was evident that the aircraft hadn't attacked the island itself. The island was oval shaped with a manmade canal that ran into the center of it then opened into a good-sized harbor. The canal was lined with steel plates to prevent erosion, and had automatic torpedo launches built in to destroy any unwanted Navy vessel that had strayed into it. There was also a large electrified fence around the shoreline, making the canal the only way onto the island. A splash appeared in front of the *Magenta's* bow. Tanks appeared on the edge of the harbor and men rushed around them.

"Unidentified armed vessel, you are in restricted waters. Disarm your weapons and prepare to surrender."

Chris nodded to the Weapons commander.

Maybe the Americans made it to shore after all, he thought. A minute passed.

"Armed vessel you need to disarm your port gun now or we fire."

Chris put on a radio headset. "We can't disarm it. It's jammed where it is."

"Chris? Is that you? Oh, man. Are we ever glad to hear from you."

How did they mistake one of their own ships for an American one?

The *Magenta* picked up speed as it turned a corner in the canal. Two huge steel doors, the island's last defense, swung open. Chris noticed a distinct lack of war ships. The *Magenta* pulled up along the shore and the crew began to leave. Chris stayed, collecting all the data he could. Soon he had an animated re-creation of the battle. The image was frightening.

Slowly icons representing ships began to disappear.

"It was horrible."

Chris jumped. He turned to see the island leader and HQ commander standing behind him. "Russell. Where's the rest of the Navy?"

Russell shook his head. "Right here," he said pointing to the *Magenta's* deck. "The *Magenta* is the only surviving ship. All the others were destroyed in the battle." Russell handed Chris a stack of papers.

"How many of the attackers made it back?"

"As far as we can tell, no aircraft did. But there were reports of some subs. We can't be sure but we think they all made it back."

Chris sat down, in shock. "We lost our whole Navy. And some of those— Wait." Chris jumped to his feet. "We destroyed one sub. Do you think sub and aircraft losses will be enough to hold the Americans back?"

Russell shook his head. "We're defenseless except for an A-10, an F-111A and an F16 that we salvaged before they went under. We have some X-A-10 and F-111 crews but I doubt they'll be effective. And we have no hope of getting a pilot for an F16. All we have are one airborne command post and a coupla choppers. We might as well have a big sign that says 'shoot me.'"

Chris's mind was running through the events of the battle trying to find a way to win. He shook his head and looked back at the papers where he recognized the name of one of the *Magenta's* designers, Tom Jones.

"Wait a second. We captured an F16 pilot. She can probably help us."

Russell laughed. "And what makes you think she'll help us?"

"It's Jessie." Chris said and rushed out the door, down the hall where he took the elevator down to the brig. He opened the door to cell 3.

"Well, well. Missing me already?" Jessie said with a smirk.

"Hardly, but I need your help again," Chris said, latching the door behind him. "But like last time, if you don't want to help... Well. I guess what happens to you is up to my CO then." His eyes swept her face, looking for clues to what she might be thinking. "We captured some US aircraft from the battle. We have a crew for two of them, but we need a pilot for the F16."

"What makes you think I'll help you fight? I want you to surrender."

Chris sighed. "Look, I know I'm no pilot but I do have friends who are. I know that in war conditions you seem to form a bond with your planes, right?"

"I admit that's pretty good. Even for a puddle pirate."

Chris suppressed a short laugh.

"We got your F16. We're fixing it up as we speak and if you want her, you can have her back. But. But you need to help us defend this island."

Jessie smiled. "You really saved her? I guess you guys aren't so bad after all." Her smile vanished. "Did they make it to the land? Did my parents survive?"

Chris sighed. "The bombers never made it to shore. Your father was out fishing. He... I'm sorry. He got caught in the crossfire."

Jessie's eyes filled with tears. "They killed my father? They'll pay for it." Jessie's upper lip curled in a snarl. "What do you need me to do?"

Chris smiled. "Fly the F16 and tell us all you can about the plan they have."

"That's easy. I was one of the head planners."

Chris looked at her, a little surprised. From what he knew, pilots were rarely involved in US military strike planning.

"The Secretary of Defense has a soft spot for me. So this is how it goes. First..." Jessie explained the whole plan to Chris. "But knowing Hurley, as soon as the President makes the call to you guys he'll press for the attack to be moved up."

Chris helped Jessie to her feet and they walked down the hall and out an open cargo door.

"Wow," Jessie exclaimed as she walked off the *Magenta*. The island was a lush tropical paradise with trees as far as the eye could see. They walked up to a lookout. From there they could see the beach, the waves crashing onto it. Chris could also see the *Magenta* and understood why the island's military hadn't recognized her. Most of her paint was gone, there were burn marks covering her and she was badly mangled, particularly on the starboard side of the bow.

"They beat that thing up pretty bad, huh?" Jessie said standing next to Chris, who nodded and pointed down off to their left.

"You did get her!" Jessie said happily. They could easily see the three aircraft parked next to a hangar and people milling around them. "What are they doing?"

"They're mounting our weapons on it. It's a safety net for us. Our weapons have self-destruct devices. They will also install one in the main part of the aircraft, most likely the wing root. This way, if any aircraft turns on us, we can destroy it in the blink of an eye."

"Good to know you trust me."

"We're battered so we can't take chances. Make no mistake though, what's left of us is still ready to fight."

"Who's this?"

Chris turned to see Russell coming up behind them.

"Ah, Russell this is Jessie Jones. Russell is the island's commander."

"I'm sorry for your loss," Russell said, holding his hand out to shake. "Your parents never mentioned how pretty you were."

Jessie smiled, blushing.

"Come now," said Russell. "We must plan for the attack."

Chris and Jessie followed Russell down into an underground command post.

"All right, so here's the plan."

White House, Situation Room

"Sir! They've answered," an aide said.

The President nodded and an image of a frazzled man appeared on the screen in front of him.

"Greetings. I'm the President of the United States."

"I know who you are," the man said sternly.

"We know you have no fighters left and that your Navy is destroyed so... We suggest that you surrender before we mount an all-out invasion of your island. We are open to negotiations."

The man on the screen laughed. "By negotiations you mean discuss how to get us off the island so you can take it."

The President nodded again but before he could say anything, the man continued. "We will not negotiate and we will not surrender."

"That is not very wise," Fredrick Hurley piped up from behind. We have the resources to take your island and there would be very high casualties if we are forced to do so."

The President shot him an angry glare. Embarrassed, Hurley sat back down.

"I'll say it again. We will not surrender. We will defend this island with our dying breath." The line went dead.

Hurley quickly rushed to the President's side. "Sir, they have done nothing short of declaring war on us. We should move the attack up and get them before they can build any makeshift defenses."

The President stayed silent for a while before rising out of his chair. "If I move it up and give you the machines and men you need, can I rest assured that you will capture the island without the same results as the last attack?" He moved to the other wall of the room.

"I would bet my pension on it sir," Hurley said confidently.

The President laughed. "Oh trust me, you are betting more than that on it."

On board the destroyer *USS Bunker Hill*

Luke looked out at the sea. It was a dark night and the sea was relatively calm. He was commanding a destroyer and was in charge of the protection of the battle group. He walked out onto the catwalk which extended out past the ship's side and over the waves. The radio on his belt beeped and a frantic voice came through.

"One F-111A. Low and fast. Nine o'clock position. Not ours!"

So much for decimated defenses. Then Luke heard the scream of jet engines. He turned to see two lights passing over a ship ahead of them. Then a huge fireball erupted, engulfing the two ships in the forward position of the battle group. Luke turned his head to avoid getting blinded and was knocked off his feet when the ship lurched sideways from the shock wave. He fumbled for his footing as alarms blared. He grabbed his radio and shouted into it.

"Battle stations, I want that thing dead!" A few seconds later he could see the forward guns swing into motion but none of them fired a shot.

"Lost contact, sir," a voice said over the radio.

Luke cursed.

"New contact. low and fast. A-10. Almost—" The voice was drowned out as the A-10 passed overhead destroying another ship. "F-111A. Low and fast. Three o'clock position."

The aircraft passed overhead nearly deafening Luke with its engine noise. Luke could smell fuel. They were using fuel explosives! Then a fireball engulfed him and it all went black.

F16 Rebel One Reaper

Jessie smiled grimly as a warship went up in flames in front of her. She yanked her fighter around as a missile lock-tone sounded. She lined up and the ship's radar disappeared from her threat detector a few seconds later. Then she saw it—an aircraft carrier. She could tell by an old bent radar tower that she had bumped into during training that it was the *USS Washington.* She fired her last two missiles at it and circled back to watch the show. The ship immediately began to list and Jessie was certain it would be on its side in a few minutes.

These weapons pack a bigger punch than anything the US has, she thought grimly before turning her fighter and heading for the island.

"Rebel One crippled one destroyer, one frigate and one carrier. I'm coming home for fuel and weapons."

"Roger that. Great job. Will turn you around as fast as we can," Russell's voice came from the radio.

She pushed her fighter low to avoid detection but it failed and a missile lock-tone sounded. She yanked her fighter left. The US ship's crew was expecting that. The missile launch warning rang out. She hit the chaff and flares buttons and put her fighter into a steep climb. The missile performed a lazy climb in an attempt to follow her. But she had to level off to avoid stalling. Another missile lock-tone sounded. The missile had found her once again. She cursed as two more missiles appeared on her threat display. She let them all get on her tail and then dove toward the ship that had launched them. She glanced at her fuel gauge. She needed to lose these guys and get back to base fast. One missile began to lag behind and exploded as it depleted its fuel supply but the others were still coming fast. She pulled up a little too late, though, and caught an antenna on the warship, ripping off one of the small stabilizers on the F16's belly. The trailing missiles plowed into the ship that had launched it, sending a shock wave through her aircraft. Once her plane was stable and she had performed a few checks, she leaned back in her chair and breathed a sigh of relief. Then her display lit up like a Christmas tree as the warning lights came on. Alarms followed, then loud explosions came from her engine. The aircraft began to shake.

"Rebel One to HQ and *Magenta* I'm ejecting," Jessie radioed before pulling her ejection handles. She felt pain in her back as she shot out of the aircraft seconds before it exploded.

On Board the frigate *USS Samuel*

George looked out in horror as a ship emerged from the water. It immediately began firing at his ship. Then, abruptly, it turned to port.

"Intersect them," he ordered. "We will be mighty popular if we capture this one. Keep an eye on their aircraft." He knew the aircraft were as great a threat as ever now that they were using fuel explosives: small flying cylinders that released fuel and "sparklers." These "sparklers" would ignite the cloud of fuel and, properly used, easily destroy two ships in a heartbeat. And the pilots definitely knew how to use them.

His ship began to turn toward the enemy when the Communications officer called out. "Sonar report mines all around us."

George was about to speak when three explosions, one after another, rocked the *Samuel.* The evacuation alarm sounded and all the men on the Bridge rushed out to the lifeboats. George ran to one of the gun posts and grabbed a grenade launcher. He could see a man standing on the deck of the enemy ship aiming what appeared to be a sniper rifle at his ship. He fired at the man but the grenade splashed into the water before it reached the other ship. In response, the enemy ship began firing once more. George ducked below a wall for safety. A crewman grabbed him.

"Sir, you must get to a lifeboat. The ship won't stay up much longer."

At that moment George realized that the deck was pitching drastically to one side. "Get to a lifeboat. I'll do as much damage as I can."

The crewman tried to speak but George swung out and took another shot. This one again fell short. He rushed to reload his weapon without thinking about ducking for cover. He looked up and the last thing he saw was the muzzle flash.

On board the gun ship *Magenta*

"Nice shot, sir," one of the *Magenta*'s gunners said in amazement.

"Thanks," Chris said, reloading his sniper rifle. Bullets coming from one of the US lifeboats sent sparks flying as they impacted the hull next to Chris. Chris swung the rifle around and pulled the trigger. A man fell out of a lifeboat as it turned away. The other was still in the fight. Chris shoved the gunner behind a wall as he fired at another lifeboat before diving for cover himself.

"Hey, Gunny, you got my extra clip?" Chris shouted over the noise of gunfire as he discharged his weapon again. The gunner slid a clip of ammunition over to him. Chris nodded his thanks and the gunner pulled out a pistol and started to shoot. The gunfire continued even though each shot Chris took found its target and as far as Chris could tell, most of the gunner's bullets had done the same. The gunfire subsided a few minutes later. Chris moved around the corner, his rifle locked and loaded. He looked over the side of the ship to see a lifeboat hugging the *Magenta*'s side. He fired a shot hitting a crewman on the lifeboat. A spray of sparks erupted by Chris's ear. He ducked for cover. When he looked back, the lifeboat was much farther away from his ship. He grabbed a grenade from his belt, pulled the clip, and threw it at the lifeboat. He didn't stay to see the result.

"Everybody below decks!" he shouted. Everyone rushed to their positions. Chris ran to a door as the *Magenta*'s bow slipped below the water. He handed his rifle to a waiting crewman and walked down the hall toward the Bridge. Without warning, the deck pitched downward more violently than usual and Chris nearly fell to the deck. After regaining his footing, Chris rushed to the Bridge door and walked into a conversation.

"... and will scuttle the ship or I will blow each and every one of your heads off myself," an engineer shouted, pointing a gun at Ian.

I don't believe it... One of my crew is helping the Americans. Chris worked his way across the wall until he found the lever that opened the EMERGENCY STOP hatch. He pushed the red button and the ship abruptly stopped, throwing Chris and the hijacker to the floor.

"What the— Chris!" The hijacker yelled as he pointed his weapon at the rising Chris.

"Miles! Why are you doing this?" Chris drew his pistol.

"That doesn't matter. Now put your weapon down. Or else."

"No. You're not shooting anyone." Chris moved to the left but Miles blocked his path.

"You wouldn't shoot me. We would all be dead if not for the failed ballast system." Miles motioned to the ballast control panel.

Chris looked away. He knew that what Miles was saying was probably true. A shot rang out and Chris's right leg was wrenched out from under him. An inferno of pain ran though his body. He looked up to see Miles had turned back to Ian.

"Override that thing and scuttle the ship or you'll be next!" Miles shouted, pointing to the emergency stop button.

Chris fought through the pain and aimed his pistol upwards.

Miles turned back to Chris. "I will not serve under the command of some—"

Chris pulled the trigger and Miles fell back, a bullet between his eyes.

For what seemed like an eternity, no one moved. Then Alex and Ian rushed to Chris's side and helped him to his seat. A medical crewman rushed over to bandage his leg.

"Are you OK, sir?" the first officer asked.

"Beside the fact that I have a bullet in my leg, I'm fine," Chris said, moving his hand to the intercom button. "Engineering, this is Bridge. Did we get any damage?"

"No, sir. She held sturdy as a rock."

"Status report," Chris said, wincing in pain as the medical crewman tightened the bandage around his leg.

"Two of the three aircraft carriers and eight US Navy ships have been sunk. Three are limping back to the US but they are listing heavily. Two subs have been destroyed and the mine field is working in our favor." Chris nodded and braced himself for what was to come next. "Our A-10 reports minor engine damage sustained flying over a ship. It's on its way back for repairs. Our F-111A is just returning to the war zone with a fresh load of weapons. And, the airborne control center reports seeing the rebel F16 exploding in mid-flight. It was too dark to see a shoot."

"We lost the F16?"

The first officer nodded.

Chris sat back in his seat and produced a heavy sigh. "How much of the US fleet is left?"

"Fewer than five ships and an unknown number of subs."

"Sir, the US President wants to talk to you," the Communications officer shouted.

"Sub, two o'clock. Our depth!"

"Open the channel for the US and make sure they can see that sub when we kill it. Weapons, when I give you the thumb's up, let 'em have it." A screen slid up beside him and the image of the US President appeared on it.

"You have tried to invade our homeland," said Chris. "As you can see, we are able to fight you off. So what is it you want now?"

The President frowned at Chris's remarks. "We are very surprised at how well-defended your island is. I must tell you now that I was foolishly misled by an official here at Washington and would like to apologize for my country's behavior."

Chris smiled. *Typical politician, always laying blame.* "I'm afraid that's not enough. You've tried to kill us and because we are not an independent nation—or a nation at all—we cannot bring you to international court, as you know. So instead, I will have you and everybody there witnesses this." He gave the thumb's up to the Weapons commander and two torpedoes shot out of the launch tube.

The frown on the face of the President of the US deepened as the torpedoes impacted the sub causing it to slip from view.

"This is what you've done to my Navy, so I will do the same to yours. However, if you make sure our location is never revealed to anyone, I will not leak this to the media of the world."

"Fine. I will recall my ships, and your location will never be revealed. I will contact your... I'll contact whoever is in charge of your island and discuss the matter further. Congratulations. You are truly a worthy adversary." The screen went black and descended.

Chris laughed. *So concerned about their careers, those guys.* "All right. Let's go hunting."

White House Situation Room

"You can't let them win. We are so close to victory. We can have them in an hour," Fredrick Hurley urged, even though he could tell the President was not impressed.

"How can you say that? We lost all but six of our ships—including the subs. The ones that got out crippled have no chance of getting to port in time and you say we can still win?" The President glared at him. "I will not give you any more men or ships to waste on this pathetic excuse for a mission. I'll talk to these people and make sure they stay hidden, understood?"

Hurley nodded.

"Good."

Just then the screen in front of them lit up with the image of a man on it. Next to the man was a list of the few remaining US ships and their condition. "Hello, Mr. President. My name is Russell and I am your equivalent on the island you are trying to take. With little success might I add."

"Very nice to hear that you're willing to talk with us," the President said. "I would first like to express our deep—"

"Chris has already filled me in on your earlier conversation. I thank you for apologizing but as you know that does very little for us." Russell's voice was calm. He was evidently trying to bury rage beneath the surface.

"Very well. We would like to know what we could do to mend this wound so the ship you have out there will stop terrorizing innocent US Navy vessels. We can negotiate now. Or at a place of your choosing. Perhaps your island?"

"As a gesture of good faith I will let you come to my island for negotiation. Come in an unarmed ship. You will be brought ashore by this island's Navy. If you bring any weapons, you will be shot. As for the remaining US ships... You have attacked our home and killed dear friends and family. Therefore, any remaining ships in the area will be considered aggressors and shall be treated as such."

"I will depart immediately."

The line went dead.

Hurley stared at the President in disbelief. "You are going to let them win?"

"I have no choice. We must make sure that this mess is cleaned up. You are coming with me. You will personally apologize to these people at the meeting. You have one hour to prepare." The President pushed past Hurley and rushed out the door. Hurley shook his head and preceded to his car where his aide waited.

"How did it go?" the aide asked as they climbed into the car.

"Not well. The President thinks we have lost, and now we are going to the island to apologize for our actions."

"What did we lose?"

Patrick Gloutney

Hurley let the divider between the driver and the rear of the car finish rising before he responded in a whisper. "We lost all but six ships and the ones that escaped are not going to make it to port in time." He slumped back in his seat. "The fact is... in a couple of days that island will be off limits."

Hurley sighed, but then smiled. "Unless..."

On board the gunship *Magenta*

They were right underneath it. When Chris looked up he could see its propellers spinning in the water. *I should shoot them right now.* The results of the last battle were better than the first but he could have done without seeing Jessie in a hospital bed with a damaged spine and a messed-up arm. "All right. Let 'em go."

Two tubes extended from the *Magenta*'s side and shot chains at the propellers of the ship above them. Soon it was dead in the water. The *Magenta* rose, breaking the surface right next to the other ship's hull. A metal gangplank was extended and Chris made his way to the mid-section of the *Magenta*. He was wearing his gun on the outside of his clothing so it was clearly visible and he had replaced the full-metal-jacket bullets he normally used with hollow-point ones. He tried his best to suppress his limp—and his anger—as he neared the door. He got to the door just as the US President was deboarding from the other ship.

The President extended his hand. "I presume your name is Chris. You can call me Bill. You have a magnificent ship."

Chris didn't accept the man's hand, instead he looked past "Bill" to the other man admiring the ship.

The President smiled. "That is Secretary of Defense Fredrick Hurley. He is also quite impressed by your ship."

"Listen. I'll be nice. But if either of you so much as spits on the floor of my ship I will put a bullet through your head." He turned. "Follow me."

Limping slightly in spite of himself, he led them to the Bridge where there

were two seats propped up next to his. "These are your seats. I hope you

enjoy the ride."

"What happened to your leg?" the President asked.

"I got shot."

The president looked at Chris as if trying to seem sympathetic but

said nothing and sat down. Hurley glared at him but Chris didn't care. "Take

us down and back to base," he said once the Americans were settled. The

bow dipped below the water and Chris enjoyed the look on the faces of the

Americans.

The ride went on noiselessly for a while before the President finally

broke the silence. "Chris. I'm very sorry about your sister. I understand she

was a hero. She left her burning battle group—"

"I know what she did and you don't need to reopen that wound,"

Chris said sternly. "My job is to escort you to and from the island. That's it."

"We appreciate your keeping us safe then," the President said.

"Oh, you aren't safe as long as I have this gun," Chris grumbled,

placing his hand on his gun and walking away.

The *Magenta* pulled into the dock and before Russell had even

gotten off the gangplank, it pulled away again. Chris followed Russell and

the President to a small room deep in the *Magenta*'s hull where they all took their seats.

"Welcome, Mr. President," said Russell. "I apologize for not having this meeting on the island but I don't think it's the safest place for you."

Chris laughed. Aside from its keeping the President away from the island, the story was also true. Most of the people who lived on the island were prepared to kill any intruder.

"We appreciate the opportunity to do this personally. And you can call me Bill." The President flashed a reassuring smile. "First off—and I know I've said this before but—we are deeply sorry for our country's action and would like to make things right with your people. We could help with salvage efforts or help protect your island until you can re-establish your defenses."

"We acknowledge your apology," Russell stated, "and the offer of helping with salvage. But we're able to keep the island well defended."

Chris nodded.

"The Secretary of Defense also has something to say to you." The President motioned for Hurley, who stood up.

"Yes," he said, clearing his throat. "I found your 'We will defend our island with our last dying breath' comment very moving and motivating. Therefore, I will fight until I die to capture this island." He grabbed a radio from his pocket but before he could use it, Russell punched him in the gut. The man stumbled backwards, dropped the radio and started swinging at

Russell. The President stood up to try to control his officer but was knocked to the floor. Russell struck Hurley in the side of the head. Hurley stumbled, spat out blood and a tooth onto the floor, reached into his coat and pulled out a pistol, aiming it at the President.

"Nobody move or the President gets it."

For a moment, no one moved. Chris, who was out of Hurley's line of vision, slowly withdrew his own pistol from its holster and fired. Hurley fell forward without half his head.

"You spat on my floor," Chris muttered angrily.

Russell and the President looked at Chris, stunned expressions on their faces.

"I warned him," Chris said, shaking his head and re-holstering his pistol. He then turned and left. Outside the room were three armed guards, their weapons drawn and plastic face covers down. They all rushed around Chris to make sure he was protected.

One of the guards began bombarding him with questions "Are you all right, sir? Are the island commander and the President all right? What about the Secretary of Defense?"

"I'm fine. So is everybody else," Chris said.

The guard looked at Chris with a puzzled expression. "Then what happened in there?"

"Oh. I shot the Secretary of Defense."

The guards turned and looked at him as if he had two heads.

Chris ignored them and continued to the Bridge. When he got there everybody stopped what they were doing and looked at him. "Plot a course to the American ship," he ordered. "I want that Yankee off my ship as soon as possible."

No one moved.

"Now!" he shouted.

With that, the whole Bridge snapped into action and the ship soon began to move forward. Chris said nothing until Russell and the President walked in. Russell motioned for Chris to follow him. Chris complied by nodding to his first officer. They walked out of the Bridge.

"You shot a high-ranking US government official to save the US President, even after they killed your sister," Russell said as soon as the Bridge door closed. "I thought you'd let the guy kill the President to give you a good reason to shoot him."

"I told you already I had a perfectly good reason to shoot the guy. He spat on the floor. I told him and the President that if they so much as spat on the floor I would kill them. I am a man of my word."

Russell laughed and shook his head. "Either way, you are now going to be a hero in the US. The President is going to send an award to you. Secretly, of course. He also said that he will cooperate with us fully. That if we ever need anything, the US will be more than happy to help."

Chris laughed. "So may I get back to commanding my ship then?"

Russell nodded, and Chris turned and walked back onto the Bridge. "How long until we reach the ship?"

"One minute, sir," the radio operator, Alex, called out. "It's still dead in the water, sir."

Chris nodded. *Those chains are doing their job.* Chris motioned to the President to follow him.

"Thank you, Chris. This ship is amazing. I'll have to come visit the island itself sometime," the President said as they walked down the hall.

"I'm sure Russell will welcome you, but as for the rest of the islanders..." Chris thought for a moment. "To put it mildly, they'll do a million times worse to you than what I did to your Secretary of Defense."

The President nodded in understanding.

"I never dreamed he'd try something like that. But he did love his job. He was committed." They reached the door. "I'll send the salvage ship to where the *Rose* supposedly was when it went under as soon as I get back." He turned and walked out the door. The door closed and the *Magenta* pulled away. Chris walked back toward the Bridge but was stopped by Russell just before he entered.

"They still have those chains on their props," Russell said, seemingly concerned.

"That's their problem, not mine." The Bridge doors slid open and

The Hidden Island

Chris walked away leaving Russell in the hallway. He took his seat and looked around the Bridge, most of which had been splattered with blood but otherwise looked normal.

"Ian. Take her down."

On board the *MV Marina*, FAR shipping vessel

Dalton Murree, walked down the halls of the old freighter. He had been with the Free Army Republic since the beginning and he had never met with the group in the same place. He walked into a room and found everyone huddled around a rather small table with the usual speakers at the head. Murree took his seat.

"I hope you bring good news, Dalton." The voice of the boss rang through clearly. The fact that every one called him by his first name was one of the many harsh reminders to Murree that he was no longer near the top when he came to these meetings.

"Unfortunately, no. The United States' attempt to capture the island failed miserably. They lost everything they sent out and declared the island off limits to any US military action. We lost one of our contacts and my brother Fredrick was also killed in the endeavor."

"I see," the boss said. "Any chance the FAR can capture the island?"

Aly said: "I have double checked Dalton's calculations and they are slim. Even if we do capture it we will have to sustain heavy casualties."

"Hang on. My calculations are based on a full-strength military. The US cut them down to one ship and two or three aircraft," Murree said.

"Was another attack launched against them?" the boss asked.

"Yes."

"And nothing made it back?" Aly asked.

"No."

"It's clear to me. There's no way we can do this. The island's not worth the lives of my men. I'm cancelling this endeavor," the boss said.

"But, sir. I am to be appointed as the Secretary of Defense in place of my brother. The Americans are in the process of developing a revolutionary aircraft that could easily take the island."

"You're just like him, Dalton. Always making sure every possibility is explored. But in this case, we can't. I'm cancelling before anything happens against us. And that is that."

"Very well."

"It has been a pleasure to work with you all. Aly, I thank you again for that perfect 747 mission. I may call on you again if you are needed. Until then, I bid you good day," the boss said, and then came the distinctive click as the line went dead.

Murree sighed and was the first to leave. He made his way out to his car and drove back to his home.

As he walked through his front door he flipped open the file on the XM-89 *Sparrow* and began to formulate a plan on how to get revenge.

Patrick Gloutney

\

A Sparrow's Dagger

Hell's Desert Aeronautical test centre, US top secret testing center

"*Sparrow 1*, you are clear to land on runway zero-eight," a voice said over the radio.

For most fighter pilots this was a welcome phrase. It meant they were safe for another day but for Henry Drape, it was a sign that the worst was yet to come. Most people would think flying one of the most advanced fighters ever built would be easy because it would do most of the flying. Unfortunately for Henry, it was quite the opposite. His fighter did help him fly, but at this point in the development, it was ultimately up to him to keep it under control.

The runway was now in sight. Henry eased the Vector Thrust Nozzle lever back a little and pulled the throttle to idle then the speed brake handle to slow the aircraft down. He set the Vector Thrust Nozzle at the 90° position and flared the aircraft's nose. Because of the raised nose, the drag acting on the plane increased and the airspeed began to drop. A bright red message appeared on his left-hand display screen:

WARNING
POOR AIRCRAFT STABILITY

This was followed by a recorded voice stating the same thing. Henry ignored it. He had failed too many times by focusing on that message. Soon the aircraft was almost hovering over the end of the runway. Henry made one quick instruments check and breathed a sigh of relief when the warning message disappeared. Then it reappeared and seconds later the left wing dropped. Henry pulled on the control stick to level the plane then realized that the throttle was still at idle. He started to push it forward but it was too late, his airspeed had dropped below ten knots. The aircraft began its inevitable spin and rolled onto its back before slamming into the runway.

Henry shielded his eyes as the hatch above him opened. He undid his restraints and pulled himself out of the simulator. Outside of the machine was the *Sparrow*'s project team, the leader of which was Henry's best friend and the commander of the Hell's Desert base, General Thomas Blume.

"I always forget something," Henry said.

"You're getting better every time you try." Thomas slapped Henry on the back. "Remember the first time you tried to take off vertically?"

Henry laughed. The first time he had tried a vertical takeoff he got about a hundred feet and then dropped like a stone.

"So let's get some lunch and we'll review the flight later."

The two men walked down to the galley. They said nothing to each other until they had finished eating.

"So," Thomas said, balling up his napkin. "Let's say you do one last run today and if it goes all right you can fly the real thing on Monday."

"They have a working prototype already?" Henry nearly spit out his coffee.

"Oh yeah. She's ready to go. Just needs a pilot. Wait'll you see her."

Henry was stunned although he wasn't sure why. "They're making fast progress. You must be really whipping them."

"Nah. I'm just along for the ride. They're a good team. Who knows? This thing could be out fighting before we know it."

Henry laughed. "I think you need to think up a better training program than a few classes and God knows how many hours on a simulator."

"At the rate you're going, we sure as hell do!" Thomas laughed. "All right, let's go review your flight, shall we?"

Back at the simulator room, they watched the whole flight, most of which was good, but then came the landing. Embarrassed, Henry shook his head. The whole thing had gone perfectly except for the throttle movement and he now noticed the warning message that had said ADVANCE THROTTLE.

"This was a great flight, Henry. Don't be too hard on yourself. Remember that in the real thing, the throttle would have been moved by the computer which would have prevented this." The screen was displaying the final few seconds of the flight.

After a short debriefing, Henry pulled Thomas aside. "Listen. I've only seen the cockpit in the simulator. Do you think I could maybe see the real thing?"

"You'll see it on Monday if this next flight of yours goes well, OK?"

Back inside the simulator, Henry strapped himself in while someone closed the hatch behind him. The screen lit up.

"All right. Here goes nothing."

On board *Golf Kilo 3*, US Transport aircraft

"What did you want to see me for?" Thomas asked as the aircraft climbed through the cloud cover.

"I'll cut to the chase," Thomas's commanding officer General Wilbert said. "The government is having second thoughts about the XM-89 *Sparrow* project."

"What? We haven't even had one test flight yet and they want to cancel the project?" Thomas looked over at the frown on his CO's face. "Or am I jumping to conclusions?"

"Not exactly cancel. They need results. The aircraft looks... different... and they don't know how well it'll fly."

"That aircraft will fly better than anything we have!"

"Well, it may fly very well but the government wants to be sure before they invest a whack of money into the project. So. This is what you are to do. You have a pilot that's ready to go, right?"

Thomas agreed.

"This pilot will get into the aircraft in broad daylight and pretend to steal it. A simulated chase will take place where he must avoid our military. He will have checkpoints where he will receive fuel. Because this is simulated, each aircraft—including the *Sparrow*—will have unlimited simulated weapons. So when we land, get your boy and get ready to start."

Although stunned by what he had just heard, Thomas quickly

responded. "Yes, sir. We will start immediately."

Hell's Desert Aeronautical test center

"Wow," Henry exclaimed as he and Thomas entered the hangar where the XM-89 *Sparrow* was sitting. "She's beautiful."

The *Sparrow* looked much like its name described it. Its two wings curved out into fine graceful points. Its fuselage was shaped like a raindrop to improve the aircraft's speed and efficiency, and it had no vertical stabilizer. Instead, it had two fins that pointed downward mounted on her tail. These would serve as both the elevator and the vertical stabilizer. As Henry brought his gaze back to the front of the aircraft, he saw that the canopy covering the *Sparrow*'s cockpit was tinted yellow. *Smart.* The yellow-tinted canopy would cut out some of the visible wavelength that created glare. He couldn't count how many times he'd had trouble tracking a target because of the glare from the sun.

Thomas pulled him under the *Sparrow*'s wing. "Now remember. You won't get shot but act as if you're going to be. The fate of this aircraft rests on your shoulders."

"Don't worry. They won't know what hit them."

"I'm not kidding," Thomas said, concerned. "You need to nail any landing you make. Here, you'll need this." He handed Henry what appeared to be a BlackBerry phone. It was black, with a keyboard on the lower portion and a figure print scanner on the back.

Henry started his way up to the cockpit then turned back to Thomas.

"Like I said. They won't know what hit them, He closed the canopy and activated the avionics.

"Hello. Welcome to the XM-89. What is your name?" The female voice of the interactive computer startled Henry.

"Henry Drape," he said.

The computer beeped in acknowledgment then spoke again: "Welcome aboard, Henry. Please state your verification number."

"One-two-eight-nine-zero-five," Henry said.

"Verified. Please place your right thumb on the blinking scanner located to your right."

Henry found the scanner and pressed his thumb against it.

"Thank you. Now hold still for facial recognition. Good. Now I will not allow anyone other than you to activate the XM-89 unless directed by you."

Henry couldn't help but laugh as he powered up. He was amazed at how quiet the engine actually was. Taxiing the *Sparrow* out of the hangar, he pulled the Vector Thrust Nozzle lever back to the 90° position then turned his head to watch as the engine rotated to the upward position. He eased the throttle forward and the *Sparrow* leapt into the air. He let the altitude increase to about two hundred feet and brought the Vector Thrust Nozzle back to the 0° position. The aircraft jolted forward and the nose swung downward. Henry quickly pulled the nose up and pushed the throttle only to realize it was already at MAX. He waited a moment before pushing the

AFTERBURNER ENABLE icon on the left-hand display screen. Within two seconds, the *Sparrow* shot from four hundred and eighty-nine knots to Mach 2, pressing Henry deep into his seat. He quickly disabled the afterburner to avoid burning excess fuel.

After five minutes of flying, the threat display showed three F16 fighters on his tail so Henry pulled back hard on his control stick and the *Sparrow* shot into a vertical climb and reached 15,000 feet in under a second. Henry rolled the aircraft and dove onto the F16s that were tailing him. He was thankful for his special load-reducing flight suit. In no time at all he had logged the *Sparrow*'s first three kills. He leveled off again but soon, another fighter and an airborne radar platform found him. He pushed the *Sparrow* lower and realized that her engine was throwing a cloud of dust. He could now see the fighter. Again, he pushed the *Sparrow* lower.

"Warning! Engine thrust creating dust cloud. Possible exposure." the computer informed him. "Fighter six o'clock. It has you."

Henry threw the thrust deflector lever back to its full-open position. The dust cloud behind him tripled in size.

"Warning. You have been detected."

The fighter tailing Henry closed the distance rapidly but Henry pressed as hard as he could on the right rudder petal. The *Sparrow* swung around and flew into the cloud of dust it had created.

"Deploy engine filters," Henry said into his microphone.

The filters came down in front of the engine air intakes, keeping small debris particles from entering the engine.

"Fighter has lost contact. Excellent flying," the computer complimented him.

Henry pulled out of the cloud of dust and shot the fighter that was tailing him, then continued on course.

"Running systems check," the computer stated. "All is in order but we are behind the fuel curve. Recommend MAX ENDURANCE."

Henry cursed.

"We have just enough to make it to the two closest checkpoints."

"Set MAX ENDURANCE and plot a course to nearest checkpoint."

A brief pause was followed by the voice of the computer: "Course set. Recommend engage auto pilot. I will keep low."

Henry reached forward to turn the Flight Direct knob to AUTO. He began to look for fighters.

The White House

"You say this guy has never flown the real thing?" asked the new US Secretary of Defense, Dalton Murree.

"That's correct," Thomas said, surprised as the image of the *Sparrow* disappeared into the dust cloud. "Nothing but simulator training. To tell you the truth, I didn't think the aircraft could do some of these maneuvers."

"I'll give you this. It flies perfectly." The Secretary of Defense turned off the video. "OK, so he should be at one of the first checkpoints now. Let's turn up the heat. I want an airborne commanded center up there so we can catch him the second he flies."

Everyone nodded. Then the meeting was dismissed.

"General Blume, may I speak with you please," asked Murree.

"Yes, Mr. Secretary?"

"I'm very impressed so far. If he makes it to the final checkpoint—and the way he's flying that doesn't look like it'll be a problem—the project will be allowed to continue. But... I would like to know more about the man flying this aircraft. I've reviewed his file and it seems he isn't just trained as a pilot. Is that true?"

"It is. He took additional combat training. If you're impressed with his flying, you should see him with a knife."

"I would like to meet him," Murree said.

Checkpoint 1-2

Henry was glad he didn't have to land a normal aircraft. The checkpoint was a small airstrip with a hangar. The runway was cracked and overgrown with weeds, and the paint was all but gone. As he approached, he could see people waiting for him in front of the hangar.

"Warning! Anti-air turrets at two o'clock and ten o'clock. They are active."

Henry pushed the throttle to MAX. The *Sparrow* leaped forward and quickly passed the airfield. Henry circled back and flew low across the airfield from the opposite direction. When he was about half way across the airfield, he yanked the Vector Thrust Nozzle lever back and the aircraft shot straight up. Henry pulled the throttle back to idle and the *Sparrow* started to fall. He then worked the throttle and lowered the gear. He touched down ten feet from the group of people watching. He then popped the canopy.

"Use caution," the computer warned as a ladder extended from the *Sparrow*'s side. Henry climbed down to be met by a man who needed no introduction. It seemed odd to Henry that Secretary of Defense Murree would come out to meet him, but he assumed it was because of the *Sparrow*, not him.

"Hello, sir," Henry said.

"I must say you really know how to handle that aircraft."

"Thank you, sir." Henry was uncomfortable as there was no good explanation as to why this man was here.

"Come with me," said the Secretary of Defense. "Let's grab a bite to eat, shall we?"

Henry was hungry so despite his worries, he agreed. He turned back to shut the *Sparrow*'s engine down when the computer suddenly spun it to a halt on its own. He followed the Secretary of Defense into the hangar where they sat at a small table and ate in silence until the Secretary of Defense broke it.

"I'm told you're not just a good pilot but also have a way with knives."

Henry was taken aback. When he had signed up for the additional training, most people laughed at him saying it would be a waste of time. To date, it had proven useless but he still enjoyed practicing. "I can throw one all right, I suppose," Henry said as he stabbed his fork into the chicken.

"Do you carry one with you all the time?" the Secretary of Defense asked.

Henry hesitated slightly before answering. "I do."

The Secretary of Defense nodded. "I would like to see you throw one."

Henry smiled. The chairs they were sitting on were wooden and the Secretary of Defense was exposing a part of the chair under his arm as he ate. Henry decided he might as well show off. With that he drew one of the two knives concealed in his boots and threw at the exposed section of the

Secretary's chair. It embedded itself perfectly into the wood leaving the man unharmed.

"I'm impressed," laughed the Secretary of Defense as he pulled the knife, with considerable effort, out of the chair. He handed it back to Henry, hilt first. "I have a proposition."

"Does the *Sparrow* survive?" Henry asked.

"Yes, yes. But I would like your help in designing some knife combat gear. You would work with Hell's Desert and would design it to work with the XM-89."

Henry took time to consider. It would be exciting to help design this type of gear and being able to continue with the *Sparrow* would be a nice bonus. "Sure," he said leaning back into his chair. "OK. I'm in."

"Don't get ahead of yourself now. If you can make it to the *Nimitz* then we'll talk."

"I'd best turn in then," Henry said and made his way to his sleeping quarters.

***

The next morning, Henry was completing his walk around the *Sparrow* when a General Scott came up to him.

"They have an airborne radar platform up there. They'll catch you as soon as you leave the ground," he said, handing papers to Henry. The Watchers, as many at Hell's Desert referred to the recon radar aircraft, could bring needed radar coverage to anywhere in the world and make it nearly impossible for a non-stealth aircraft to pass undetected under the Watchers' eyes. Although they were never armed, they could direct a fighter to a target without giving the target any warning.

"Oh, um. Well then..." Henry fumbled as he tried to come up with a solution. "Hang on. Let me try something." Henry climbed into the *Sparrow's* cockpit.

"Hello. Welcome to the XM-89. Please present your right thumb for scanning," the computer said.

Henry did as he was told.

"Hello, Henry," the computer said, after the verification process was finished.

"Can you plan solutions to problems?" Henry asked.

"I am able to plan solutions if they are air-battle based."

"We have an airborne radar platform and four F16s up there and..." Henry read all the information off the papers.

After a brief silence, the computer responded. "What other aircraft are available to you?"

Henry relayed the question down to the General.

"We have a couple of F15s and some F18s but that's it."

Henry was about to relay this message to the computer but it had obviously heard the reply. "Are these aircraft battle-ready?"

Henry again played messenger between the aircraft and the General, this lasted about two minutes.

"This is the best possible solution," the computer said finally, displaying information and simulation for Henry to review. What Henry saw made him smile.

On board *Zulu 4*

"One new contact low and fast bearing two-five-six. *Zulu Three* and *Four* proceed and investigate. *Zulu One* and *Two* stay back and protect BASKET."

Dave smiled. He always thought "BASKET" was a stupid code name for the airborne radar platforms but he still enjoyed hearing it over the radio. He pulled away and he and his leader went after the contact.

"New contact low and fast bearing one-five-six. *Zulu Three* proceed and investigate."

The aircraft next to Dave peeled away.

Dave continued following directions from the airborne radar platform so as not to be detected by the contact. After a few minutes he was rewarded with a black speck off in the distance. He pushed his throttle forward and closed the final few miles. When he saw what it was he slumped back in his chair.

"BASKET, this is *Zulu Four*. It's an F15." Dave pulled his aircraft away and started to head back to the airborne radar platform.

"*Zulu Three* is dead. I repeat. *Zulu Three* is dead. All fighters regroup and protect BASKET."

Dave pushed his plane faster.

"*Zulu One* is dead. *Zulu Two* is dead." The voice of the controller was growing more and more frantic by the second.

Jeez. Doesn't he know this is all fake? Then Dave saw it. It was like a missile flying at a vertical angle heading right for BASKET.

"BASKET is dead," the controller said and the line went silent.

Dave dove after the now-fleeing fighter. He was soon on its tail and was about to get a lock on, when it moved lower. Dave followed it and they were soon circling a lake.

What's he doing? Just then the tail of the aircraft seemed to grow and water went spraying up, raining down on Dave's F16 like one long continuous wave. Then Dave heard his engine sputter. He cursed as he pulled his aircraft up above the flying water. Once his engine began to run normally again, he glanced around for the enemy. It didn't take long to find him. Before Dave knew it, a missile lock-tone sounded. He cursed the pilot of the enemy aircraft and radioed in.

"*Zulu Four*'s dead."

Just outside checkpoint 2-4,

Four figures moved stealthily to the edge of the bush. Kansas knew the second that they left the bush they would lose all their cover. They were under the orders of the Secretary of Defense to try to steal the XM-89 *Sparrow*. It was all a simulation after all, but he didn't want to lose the game.

"Move! Move! Move!" Kansas rasped. The four men rushed to the side of the hangar. One of them placed a small device on the code lock and the door clicked open. The men rushed inside and closed the door behind them.

Kansas and the rest of the team stopped in their tracks when they saw the XM-89 *Sparrow*.

"Wow," Kansas heard someone say.

"Make sure to fill the cannons. Move!"

While two of Kansas's men ran to fill the cannons, he and the fourth man made their way to the side of the aircraft. The man with Kansas was to fly the aircraft, so quickly climbed into the cockpit. Kansas reached the cockpit just as his pilot flipped a switch on the control panel.

"Hello. Welcome to the XM-89. Please scan right-hand thumb."

Kansas nodded to the pilot who did so.

"Thank you."

The canopy of the aircraft slammed down pinning the fingertips of Kansas's gloves underneath it. Kansas bit his lower lip to keep himself from yelling out in surprise. He tore off his gloves. Much to his relief, his fingers were still intact. "What the hell are you trying to do?" he half shouted, half whispered angrily to the pilot inside the aircraft who was banging on the canopy.

"I can't open it. It's locked."

"Never mind! Start the engine and let's get out of here," Kansas said, annoyed.

"I tried. No dice."

Just then, the canopy opened. Kansas ordered the pilot to try again.

"US Air Force! Hands where I can see 'em," someone yelled from across the hangar.

Kansas cursed. They'd been made. "Start it and get out of here!" he ordered, but the aircraft's engine remained silent.

Once the two men were on the ground, they opened fire at the American. Suddenly the aircraft's landing lights snapped on.

"Damn plane," Kansas muttered as he stumbled back shielding his eyes.

"I'm out," one of the men under the starboard wing called. The men wore vests that detected laser beams from another gun to determine if they were shot or not.

Kansas looked off to his left to see another one of his men using the landing gear as protection. Kansas aimed his gun and fired but had to back away as the aircraft lit up again. Growling, he returned fire. After a few more attempts he crouched behind a toolbox and slipped his last simulated mag into his gun. He swung out again and fired his last rounds at the figure standing at the other side of the hangar.

The figure grabbed his shoulder and fell backwards out of sight.

Kansas smiled. This guy was going all out and he liked it when that happened. He turned to his men.

"Now get the plane out of here!" he shouted and looked over at the aircraft. The last thing he saw were muzzle flashes off the aircraft's nose.

Hangar 1 at checkpoint 2-4

Henry fell back muttering to himself. The vest told him he'd been shot in the shoulder. Nothing fatal. However he was now not allowed to use that arm—his good arm—to shoot. Then he heard more gunshots, but louder this time. He grabbed his gun with his left hand and swung out to see the *Sparrow*'s air-to-air combat cannon shoot the last man standing. Then the door behind Henry swung open.

"Well done, boy," Secretary of Defense Murree said. "That aircraft is just full of surprises. How did you know they'd try it tonight?"

"Always expect the unexpected. Gas up the *Sparrow*. I'm leaving NOW!" Henry wanted out of there and to the *Nimitz* before the other players tried anything else.

Murree shouted the order to the guards and soon the *Sparrow* was ready to go.

Henry climbed into her cockpit and went through the verification process. "Thanks for saving me," Henry said as he started the engine.

"I am a machine. I do not perform selfless acts. I did what I did in self-defense. Sorry to disappoint you."

"OK. If so, how can you be sorry?"

There was no response from the computer.

"I think there's more to your programming than meets the eye." Henry pushed the throttle and the aircraft lurched forward.

"There are fighters up there," the computer said as the aircraft lifted off the ground.

Henry moved the Vector Thrust Nozzle lever forward and pushed the aircraft low.

"Search radar three o'clock. Two more at five o'clock. They are changing to tracking radar."

"Let's show them what we can do," Henry said and he yanked the aircraft right. The Secretary of Defense was pulling out all the stops to test the *Sparrow*, it seemed, and Henry wasn't going to lose this war.

"They are following. They are now at our altitude."

Henry smiled as a lake came into view. He pushed the aircraft low to the water and luckily the fighter pilot did the same. Henry threw the Thrust Deflector lever back and looked to see the fighter pulling away. The threat detection system on the *Sparrow* displayed it as downed. Henry smiled as brought the *Sparrow* up.

"Fighter count," he demanded.

"Five. Missile launch. Ejecting chaff and flares."

Henry put the *Sparrow* into a sharp bank and pulled it around until he saw the aircraft that had launched the missile. *Gotcha.* "Lock missile." A triangular icon appeared on the Overhead Display and landed on the fighter. "Fire."

A simulated missile sped away from the *Sparrow*. The aircraft banked away exposing its belly to the missile that would have plowed right into it causing a huge fireball if it had been real. Henry pushed the throttle to MAX and pointed the *Sparrow* toward the planned checkpoint.

"Set MAX ENDURANCE."

The computer replied with a beep.

The enemy fighter peeled away.

Outta gas, Henry thought happily.

On board *Sparrow 1*

"Running systems check. All is in order. We have sufficient fuel to reach the *Nimitz*," the computer reported.

Henry's smile widened. "Excellent. Vectors to *Nimitz*?" He was proud of himself and of the *Sparrow*. They had escaped the US military in mere days. Even with the limited range, the *Sparrow* had proven itself. Now there was only one thing left to test: Landing on an aircraft carrier on a windy day.

"Turn heading two-seven-two."

Henry did so and then cued his radio. "*Sparrow 1* to *Nimitz*. Do you read me?"

"Henry, it's Thomas. It's good to hear your voice. What's your status?"

"All's well. We're on course to rendezvous."

"Winds are strong. Be careful."

"Duly noted." Henry said. "You sit tight I'll be there soon." Shaking his head, he sat back in his seat. He had to make an impression with this landing. A real impression.

It took only a few minutes for the *Nimitz* to come into view. Henry pulled the *Sparrow* up so it would be level with *Nimitz*'s deck and when he was sure everyone on the Aircraft Carrier could see him, he put the *Sparrow* into another vertical climb. When he reached 1500 feet he pushed the nose back down and pulled the throttle to idle. When the nose fell back earthward, the *Nimitz* was right in its path. At the last second before the

Sparrow was about to plow into the deck, Henry pulled her level. Once he got far enough away from the *Nimitz* again, he pressed hard on the left rudder petal and the aircraft spun around on approach to *Nimitz*'s deck. Henry pulled back the Vector Thrust Nozzle lever and smiled. *I'll bet that stirred things up a bit.*

Then a warning message appeared and the computer called out. "Warning. High cross wind. Warning. Loss of control possible."

Henry cursed and continued his approach.

"Recommend abort. Request *Nimitz* change position."

"No. If I want to keep you flying we need to be able to land in any conditions," Henry said sternly. As he approached, the wind forced the aircraft sideways. It was getting harder to control. Finally they were hovering over *Nimitz*'s deck but every attempt to reduce power resulted in the aircraft's sliding to the right.

"Do not attempt a landing. Warning. Do not attempt a landing."

Henry was about to give in when he thought of something. "Oh yeah? Watch this." He pressed the left rudder pedal to the floor and pulled the throttle back to thirty percent. The aircraft's nose swung left and stayed steady for a second then began sliding backwards. Henry pushed the nose down a few degrees and reduced the power further. Soon they were only a few feet from the deck. Henry threw the throttle to idle and pressed the right rudder pedal to the floor. The nose swung around and the *Sparrow* touched down facing the *Nimitz*'s bow. Henry smiled and taxied toward the elevator.

"Nice flying. I never would have thought of that."

"You think too much like a computer. You need to be a pilot," Henry said as he parked the *Sparrow* on the elevator that began to lower into the hangar under the flight deck. When it cleared the flight deck, he saw a company of marines waiting for him.

"My, we are popular," the computer said.

Henry laughed, taxied off the elevator and followed the air marshal's instructions to his parking space. He began shutting the *Sparrow* down but left the avionics on. He climbed out of the cockpit and down the ladder.

Thomas rushed up to him. "Man, you are amazing with that thing. No one thought you were going to make that landing. In fact, the Captain was just waiting for you to ask him to turn."

Henry laughed. "Look who showed up." The Secretary of Defense was standing just behind Thomas. "I hope you liked the show, Mr. Secretary," Henry said, shaking his hand.

"Liked it? It was the best damn piece of flying I've ever seen!" The Secretary of Defense said laughing. "You, my boy, are going to be flying that thing for the rest of your career and you are going to help train the new pilots."

Henry smiled. The project was going to live.

With that, the Secretary was rushed off the deck and the crew was ordered back to work.

Henry turned to the *Sparrow* to climb the ladder to the cockpit. "Thanks," he said quietly.

"You are welcome. See you tomorrow?"

Henry chuckled and turned the avionics off. He walked to the door leading to the rest of the ship.

"Yeah. See you tomorrow," he said as he turned the light off.

Hell's Desert aeronautical test center, one year later

"OK, Henry. Let's see what you can do." Thomas placed a helmet on Henry's head. "This helmet is designed to create a 3D world around you, to simulate battle scenarios. You're going to be testing the knife combat gear that you helped design by request of the Secretary of Defense."

A few seconds passed before it kicked in but when it did, Henry was amazed at the realism of the image.

"OK, now, here comes the enemy," Henry heard someone say and sure enough the images of four people appeared around him. He quickly flexed his wrists downward and blades shot out of black devices on each of Henry's forearms. He moved forward and slashed the man standing in front of him. Bullets flew. He spun around snatching a throwing knife from a holster on his upper left leg. He tossed this at one of the gunners and it sliced through the gun and into the man's chest. Henry spun around throwing another knife at a second man. He threw a bent blade at a third man and this blade sliced through the man's throat and circled back hitting the fourth man. Henry got the last man by kicking him in the side with a cyanide-laced blade that extended from the toe of his boot. The man fell to the ground, shaking, gasping for breath. A few seconds afterwards, the image dissolved and someone lifted the helmet off Henry's head. Henry was impressed by how strategically every blade had been situated on the combat uniform. There were four lightweight blades in holsters arranged in an X on the straps across his chest, four on each leg, and two each on his arms above the elbow. All the blades were placed so they moved with him and were never getting in the way.

"That, my friend, was amazing," Thomas said. "I knew you could fight with blades but had no idea you were that good."

Henry was pleased with himself and with the praise. It had been a year since his fight to save the *Sparrow* project. In the past year the aircraft had undergone many changes, but there was still only one *Sparrow* in existence.

"The gear helped," Henry said.

"Yeah, right. Sure it did," Thomas responded, laughing. Then Thomas's phone rang. "Go get changed. I'll meet up with you later."

Henry proceeded to the locker room.

When Thomas came out of his office he walked up to Henry with a puzzled expression on his face. He motioned for Henry to follow him into a secure room.

"The Brass has an assignment for you," Thomas said once the room was secure. "Have you heard about operation IRON WATER?"

"Rumors. I heard that a bunch of A-10s and some of our Navy went out to attack an island and none came back? Why?"

"Those rumors have just been confirmed. You are to take the *Sparrow* and assassinate the head of that island's Navy. You are also to take the knife combat gear." Thomas smiled. "That's all they'd tell me but they said you'll need to find the island's ship—it's called the *Magenta*—by yourself."

"Order's been verified?" At Thomas's nod, Henry said, "OK. But I'm going to need fuel along the way."

"They have you covered and the *Sparrow*'s is being fueled as we speak."

The two men walked to the hangar where the *Sparrow* was parked. Henry started up the ladder.

Here goes nothing.

On board the *Magenta*

The *Magenta*'s dive leveled as the Bridge filled with smoke. Alarms rang out all around the ship. Chris appraised the three dimensional display of the vessel. Most of the image was red. The damage was widespread. "Engineering. Damage report."

"It ain't good, Captain." Chris sensed fear in the Chief's voice. "That last shot set both transformers on fire. The reactors are about to do the same. We have gallons of water pouring in."

"Sir," the First Officer added. "There's reports of flooding in Cargos 2 and 4. And Weapons reports flooding in Sections 1 and 5."

That was not what Chris wanted to hear. "Surface and abandon ship," he ordered.

Ian called out: "Controls are not responding."

Chris tried to shout "Emergency blow," but his throat filled with smoke and it came out more like a cough.

"No response," Ian coughed back.

"Implement underwater evacuation protocol," the First Officer repeated. On Chris's control panel, red lights flashed followed by a high-pitched alarm. Everyone on the Bridge rushed to the exit.

"Let's go! Let's go! Get out!" Chris shouted as people rushed toward the three airlocks on board.

Once everyone was safely enclosed in two of the airlocks, Chris and the First Officer entered the third. Chris spun the locking wheel until it clicked and a green light indicated the closure was secure. They grabbed the two respirators on the wall just before the ship lurched sideways. The First Officer opened the airlock door and as water rushed in, they swam through the door.

Chris broke the water's surface and swam toward one of the lifeboats previously ejected with the first groups that had evacuated. The lifeboats kept their distance to avoid the downward current that the sinking ship created. As the crew members hauled him in, Chris grabbed a waterproof walkie-talkie.

Chris pressed a button on his watch. "Well done, everyone. Best drill we've ever had." In seconds the *Magenta* resurfaced and the lifeboats rode alongside her. Ramps extended from the deck and Chris made his way up to the Bridge. Ian was the last to arrive.

"Ian," he said, trying his best to sound angry. Everyone on the Bridge stared, seemingly surprised. "Take us home."

Ian appeared relieved and everyone on the Bridge laughed.

It took ten minutes to reach the entrance to the island harbor, which now looked like a graveyard. Vessels that had been destroyed in the Americans' attempt to take the island two years previously lay on the island's shores. Some simply had holes in them while others were nothing but bits and pieces. The plan was to leave two ships on either side of the harbor entrance in their damaged state as memorials. The rest would be repaired or used for spare parts. However, the Americans had been ruthless, causing heavy damage to almost every ship on the shore, and severely crippling the small air force. Because the *Magenta* had proven it could defend the island on its own, the Navy had fallen to a lower priority on the list of repairs. The repairs would take time—if completed at all.

"Sir, we are nearing the *Rose*," the First Officer said.

"You have the Bridge." Chris walked away down the hall and out onto the deck to the railing. The starboard side of the *Magenta* had been repaired but was still badly dented and scraped from when it had hit the sea floor in the Great Battle.

Ahead, they would pass the *Village Bound* just before they reached the *Rose*. Even after two years, the image of the *Village Bound* sinking along with the last survivors of the *Rose*'s battle group, was still fresh in his mind. Chris turned and ran his hand across the partition behind him. The *Magenta* was a symbol of hope for the islanders. It had survived the Great Battle, and to Chris, it was now more his home than the island was. Since the battle, he had been living on board the *Magenta*. He had volunteered his house for Jessie to stay in until they could spare the resources to build her one of her own. He had spent the night there a few times when the *Magenta* had been dry-docked but had always felt better on board the ship. He took one last glance toward the shore as the *Rose* slipped past and then made his way back to the Bridge.

"Are you okay, sir?" the First Officer asked.

"I'm fine," said Chris, seating himself. "Let's get this thing docked so we can reload."

The First Officer nodded, gave the command and in no time, they were docked and the crew had begun to disembark.

Chris was the last to leave the Bridge. He was met by Russell.

"How'd it go?" Russell asked as they descended the gangplank.

"The crew has it down pat. I'm gonna take off but I'll be back in time to take her out again. If that's all right with you?"

Russell nodded and Chris walked over to one of the four-wheelers parked beside a helicopter hangar.

"Chris!" Chris turned to see Jessie walking up to him.

"Oh. Um. This'll be quick," Jessie said once she got to him.

Chris suppressed a laugh.

"The VTOLs want to test out that new landing pad as soon as possible so they want to know if it's finished."

"Far's I know it's not, but I'll let you guys know soon as, OK?" Chris climbed onto the four-wheeler. "Is there a reason you're asking me and not the helicopter commanders?"

"No reason," she said, and winked.

Chris grinned as he started up the four-wheeler.

"Oh. Best the south way," Jessie advised. "The north way's really muddy."

"Thanks." Chris gunned the throttle.

He drove for nearly a quarter of an hour before cresting a hill to see what was left of the *Rose* on the shore with the white tombstones in front of her. The ship lay on its side in two pieces. He rode alongside and shut the four-wheeler off. As he walked alongside the vessel, he ran his hand along its shattered keel. The island investigator had concluded that an anti-ship missile had hit her dead center before she went down. Chris climbed onto the dead ship and made his way to the Bridge. They had also concluded a malfunctioning missile had torn most of the partitions and ceilings off. He climbed into the Bridge and sat down beside the captain's chair, his dead sister's chair. His throat tightened as he fought back tears. Pulling his pistol from its holster, he saluted, and fired one shot into the sky.

After a moment, Chris climbed out of the *Rose* and made his way to another pile of metal. This was all that was left of Jessie's F16. Chris was glad that she had escaped the doomed plane.

As he turned away, he heard an alarm in the distance.

An air strike! He ran to the four-wheeler, climbed on and turned the key. The engine turned over briefly, then sputtered and died. "Come on!" Chris swore and tried again only to get the same result. He pressed the activate button on the locator on his belt and at a controlled run, he headed for the shoreline.

He could see the *Magenta* coming around the bend. It pulled up along the edge of the island's channel. Chris ran up the gangplank and the door slid shut behind him.

Washington International Airport

Dalton Murree climbed into the back seat of a black sedan. The car pulled away before he had even closed the door. "Are you nuts?" he shouted at the driver.

"I apologize for my driver. He was a last-minute replacement."

Murree glared at the figure sitting next to him. "Never mind that. Are you up to the job?"

"Flying *Marine One* is a piece of cake, but I'm not exactly sure what else you want me to do," the woman answered.

"I need you to destroy the dummy helicopters and crash land *Marine One*. You know, to make it look like an accident. Well? Can you do it?"

The woman was obviously not impressed.

"Look. I'm not asking you to commit suicide. I'll be in the 'copter, too, so it needs to land soft enough for both of us to survive."

"*Marine One* is a delicate aircraft. You can't just expect it to hold together if it crashes."

"I know, I know. But for the plan to work, I have to appear to be in danger as well." Murree was getting annoyed. "If you're not up to the challenge, I'll find another pilot..."

"I didn't say I'd be unable to do it. I'm saying I can't guarantee success. No pilot could guarantee pulling something like that off."

"You'll do just fine. Come on. Let's get you ready for the swap."

The Hidden Island

Murree reached for the door handle as the car pulled up in front of a hangar.

Inside the hangar were *Marine One* and two other helicopters that were used to conceal *Marine One*'s identity from threat.

"Hello, sir," a voice called from the other side of the hangar.

Murree turned to find a pilot—a pilot who doubled as a mechanic—walking toward them, wiping his hands on an oil-stained rag. "Al. Nice to see you again. How are the choppers?"

"Good. Always good. Who have you got with you?"

"Renée is your new relief pilot." They shook hands. "Anyone else here?"

"Just me. I'm putting the birds to bed. If you know what I mean." Al said laughing.

"That's great." Murree pulled a .45 caliber pistol out from under his coat. He fired three shots into Al's chest. "Sorry but I have a schedule to keep."

On board *Sparrow 1*

"Roger, *Deville 243*. Thanks for the gas," Henry said as he reduced power to put more distance between the two aircrafts. He had been flying in formation with the KC-10 for about three hours and it was becoming second nature for him to perform an air-refueling. The KC-10 was not just being used as a fuel supply, but Henry was flying as close as possible so radar would take him and the converted DC-10 as one aircraft.

"How much information do we have on this Chris guy?" Henry asked the computer.

"Not much. We know that he is the commander of a small Navy. We also know that he is in command of a state-of-the-art gunship called the *Magenta* that can submerge itself like a submarine. The United States attacked the island he lives on and he was part of the resistance. We lost the battle with heavy casualties and the President visited the island to make a formal apology. We have since provided salvage equipment but they would not allow us to help in the salvage efforts."

"That's it? And now they want him dead?" Henry sighed, shaking his head. "All right then. When do we enter their airspace?"

"Two minutes."

Sure enough, exactly two minutes later a radio transmission came through: "KC-10 tanker and unidentified aircraft. You have entered restricted airspace and we have detected weapons. Turn back now or prepare to be fired upon."

Henry ignored the warning and the two aircrafts continued on course. *So much for the plan.*

"Run a radar sweep. Try to find the target ship."

The computer acknowledged Henry's order with a beep.

"It is at our two o'clock about fifteen miles. It is traveling at sixteen knots."

Then Henry saw the missile, a black dart. Unfortunately, Henry had only caught a glimpse of it before it plowed into the tail section of the KC-10. Henry yanked the *Sparrow* away before the explosion engulfed her, too. He circled back in time to see the KC-10 spinning downward.

"*Sparrow 1* to base. *Deville 243* is hit. I repeat, *Deville 243* is hit. I see 'chutes." Henry pushed the *Sparrow* low to the water and headed for the target. "Distance to target?"

"Ten miles and closing fast."

"Keep calling it," Henry ordered as he turned on the auto pilot. He undid his restraints then reached for a respirator and loosened his lightweight, flexible knife combat suit which doubled as a flight suit.

"Five miles. Four miles. Three miles. Two miles. One mile..."

Henry could see the ship now. It was badly beaten but still looked pretty cool. "Prepare for dump." The ship began to shoot at the *Sparrow* but she continued on course performing only minor jigs to avoid getting hit.

When she was within a quarter of a mile of the ship, she inverted and the canopy swung open. Henry slid out of the *Sparrow* as it passed over the ship. He threw a grappling hook and it wrapped around a support beam so he could swing himself onto the deck. Instantly, men began throwing themselves at Henry. Henry grabbed one of them, flipped him, and pulled a gas grenade from his belt. He pulled the pin and threw it along the floor. The potent gas filled the air, knocking out anyone it reached, making it easier for Henry to execute his orders.

He ran below decks only to be greeted by armed guards. He threw another gas grenade before continuing. After a few twists and turns running through the ship's halls, Henry jumped back as a spray of bullets pelted the floor next to him. He looked around the corner to see two motion-sensing Gatling guns pointed in his direction.

Great. He stood there for close to forty-five seconds before drawing two knives from his pocket and flipping them open. He swung out and ran down the hall, throwing his knives at the guns. One of the bullets just missed Henry's left ear. He ducked and rolled past the guns. He looked back expecting to see them swiveling around to shoot him but much to his delight, his knives had jammed the guns in their original position. Smiling, Henry continued down the hall.

He encountered another group of guards but none had respirators on. His gas grenades quickly dealt with them. The door to the Bridge slid open. There, facing out at the water, was his target. He quickly drew a knife when the man turned and shot an electrical panel next to Henry with his pistol. The heat of the sparks that few off it stunned Henry enough that when he threw his blade, it flew way off target to imbed itself in a console.

"Of course, you're American," the man said, clearly disgusted.

Henry frowned and threw another blade at the man as the man fired a second shot. Henry's blade struck the man's left shoulder and the man's bullet did the same to Henry's shoulder. Henry grunted in pain but kept the fight going. He threw a serrated blade at the man who jumped aside but not quickly enough as the blade nicked his abdomen. The man fired again. Henry tried to avoid it only to have it graze his own abdomen.

"You know, most people prefer guns," the man said, clutching his stomach.

Henry threw his last two knives. The first one reached its target: the man's one good shoulder, and the other sliced into his kneecap. Falling, the man fired off two more shots. The first hit Henry in the forearm and the second wrenched his leg out from under him. The two men lay there motionless, red warning lights flashing overhead.

"We could keep this up 'til were both dead or we could call a truce," the man said.

"I'm sure you'd like that," Henry spat. "You live and I die of my injuries."

"I promise you'll will be treated the same way I will be. I could use someone like you on this ship."

Henry grunted in disgust. "And what makes you think I'm going to help you."

"Just a feeling."

White House Situation Room

"This can't be good," the President said, the group in the room acknowledging him with nods and grunts.

"And it isn't, sir," Thomas said. "Normally our satellites are unable to read anything over this specific portion of the Pacific Ocean but yesterday we were able to capture these images." Thomas pressed the play button on a remote and the images of a KC-10 exploding appeared. "We don't know what caused the explosion but we assume enemy fire." The video continued displaying the *Sparrow* flipping onto its back before the image froze.

"What was your pilot doing in that airspace?" the President asked. "That area's restricted."

"Sir? He was following an assassination order he received from you a few days ago." Thomas suddenly had a bad feeling and his worst fears were confirmed when the President said:

"I gave no such order."

Great! Things just got very, very interesting. "Then... If I may ask... Who did, sir?" Thomas looked around the room but no one seemed to know anything about it.

"We'll deal with that later. Have you made contact with the pilot since this happened?"

Thomas shook his head. "No sir, but as you can see..." Thomas backed the image up to that of the KC-10 going down and pointed to orange objects in the bottom right-hand corner of the image. "Parachutes, sir. The crew of the tanker could still be alive."

"I would like to personally go and help with the rescue effort, Mr. President," Dalton Murree, the Secretary of Defense, offered.

"Good. Depart immediately," said the President, stern faced. "And as for the rest of you? You're all dismissed. Except for Thomas. Er, General Blume."

When they were alone, the President continued. "These people are dangerous. They destroyed multiple warships with only three planes and one gunship. We cannot have them retaliating to this."

"I know, sir. I might be able to provide more insight if I knew what it was exactly that happened a couple years ago." Thomas smiled at the President.

"You are dismissed," the President said firmly.

Thomas nodded, saluted and left.

Sailing Sands Airfield

Murree pulled his thumb across his throat to signal the pilot to shut the big search-and-rescue helicopter down. After the blades swung to a stop, Renée climbed out, obviously not impressed.

"Change of plans," Murree called. "We have one more witness to take care of. You know what to do."

Renée nodded cursing him. "May /shoot this one?"

Murree nodded and she made her way to the hangar as headlights came around the turn. The car pulled into the parking lot a few moments later.

"I'm Walter Gustafson. General Blume's aide. You have something for him?" The man flashed his ID at Murree.

"Come with me," Murree said. "It's just in here." He opened the door and Walter entered the hangar. Murree followed.

"What is this, some kind of joke? There's nothing here!" Walter turned.

Murree punched him in the face. Walter staggered to the floor but quickly jumped back up and hit Murree in the gut. Murree tried to hit back but got a fist to the face instead. He fell but before he could rise, he looked up to see Walter with his pistol drawn.

"Hands where I can see 'em!" Walter yelled.

"Thomas has taught you well," Murree grunted, wiping blood from his chin.

"Not to be disrespectful, but General Blume can't fight to save his life. Henry taught me. Now show me your hands." Walter cocked the hammer on his gun.

"Too bad you didn't pay more attention in your classes."

From behind, Renée tackled Walter who let a shot fly on the way down to the floor but it missed both Murree and Renée.

"Nice work, Renée. Now help me restrain him." With Renée's help, Murree wrestled Walter into a chair where Renée tied ropes around his arms and legs.

All the while she kept grumbling. "He should just let me shoot him and get things over with,"

"Sorry we couldn't have met under more pleasant circumstances," Murree said, leaning down and staring into Walter's eyes, "but I need to know everything your boss knows about that assassination order."

Walter's response was a head shake.

"Let me make myself clear." Murree moved his face so it was mere inches from Walter's. "What does your boss know? Tell me or die."

Walter head-butted Murree in the face.

Murree stumbled back clutching his nose. "All right. Renée."

Renée looked up from the weapon she was loading.

"Show our guest the weapon we plan to use for his execution."

"With pleasure." Renée raised her weapon and fired a shot at a wooden box. On impact, the bullet disintegrated the box in a fury of fire.

"Exploding bullets. Courtesy of your boss's test center. Effective if placed well, but I bet they'd hurt like crazy in the arm."

"All he knows is that the order was false," Walter offered, glancing over at Renée's weapon. "He doesn't know who sent it."

Murree shot him an angry glare.

Walter squirmed.

Then Murree nodded to Renée who raised her weapon.

"I swear he knows nothing else!"

Murree raised his hand and Renée sighed, lowering her weapon.

"You know what?" said Murree. "I actually believe you."

Some of the tenseness eased from Walter's shoulders

"Too bad my .45 doesn't." Murree pulled the .45 out of his coat and fired one shot into Walter's head execution style.

A grunt from Renée made him turn around..

"You said I could shoot this one!"

On board US SAR helicopter 2324

"So let me get this straight. You are shooting these guys, too?" Renée snarled. "When do I get to kill someone?"

"For now you don't get to kill anyone. You need to establish a clean reputation for the plan to work." Murree scanned the water for the missing crew members.

Renée rolled her eyes. "How long do I stay undercover?"

"A year or so. Just long enough for the President to trust you."

A voice came over the radio: "Unidentified helicopter. You have entered restricted airspace. Turn back now or prepare to be fired upon."

Murree cued the radio.

"We are on a search and rescue mission to get a KC-10 tanker crew that was shot down."

"Roger. We know the crew you are speaking of. Turn right heading one-zero-nine," the voice said.

They followed the directions and soon they could see the life raft about twelve feet ahead of them. Murree made his way to the back of the chopper and clipped his harness to the repelling line. He opened the door and looked down to the water. By now the chopper was hovering over the life raft. Murree threw the repelling line down and slipped on a pair of heavy gloves. He jumped out of the helicopter and slide down the line. He stopped himself three feet above the raft.

"How are you gentlemen?" he asked.

"Better now that you're here, sir," one of the men said.

"So what happened to you guys?"

"We don't know. We were flying with that secret plane and next thing we know our tail's gone and were spinning towards the ocean," a second man said.

"I take it the boom operator didn't make it," Murree said, opening a pouch in his repelling gear.

"That's right, sir," the first man said.

"Here." Murree tossed down water to the men in the raft.

"Thank you, sir," the third man said.

"Don't thank me yet." Murree drew his pistol. The third man tried to retaliate by throwing the water canteen at Murree but Murree shot him dead then fired one shot at each of the other men. Two more shots went into the life raft which hissed in protest. Murree pressed his remote and the repelling line retracted slowly.

When Murree was half way up, the chopper sawed sideways nearly causing him to lose his grip on the repelling line. "Keep it steady!"

Murree ignored the muffled response from the cockpit but once he was in the chopper he went to where he and Renée had stored the bodies of Al and General Blume's assistants. Grasping the bodies, he dragged them to the door in time to see the life raft slipping below the water. He threw the two bodies out of the chopper, closed the door and made his way to the cockpit.

"I should shoot you right now," Renée said as Murree did up his restraints.

"You'll get to shoot somebody in good time. Don't you worry."

Serenidad

Chris grunted in pain as Jessie helped him into his wheelchair. He hated this. Being pushed around like he was incapable. He hated it even more that Jessie was doing it. She had insisted after he had wheeled her around for the time she had spent in the chair after the Great Battle.

"You ready?" she asked.

Chris nodded.

With that, she wheeled him down the hall and into a small black room inside which sat the man who had attacked him.

"I was beginning to wonder when you were going to get here," Henry said. He too was in a wheelchair. Chris had kept his word. Henry had been treated the same way he had only he had been in handcuffs most of the time. Jessie rolled Chris to the table then took a seat in the far corner of the room.

"I'll get to the point," Chris said. "Why did you try to kill me?"

"Orders."

Chris slowly pulled his pistol from its holster. Then wincing from the pain in his shoulder, he placed it on the table in clear view.

"I'll ask again. Why were you trying to kill me?"

Henry didn't respond.

"Very well. Jessie?"

Jessie rose to circle around behind Henry, running her hand across his beaten shoulder and drawing her own weapon and placing it to Henry's neck.

"Talk or I shoot," she commanded.

Chris was rather enjoying this, more than he wanted to.

"Shoot me then," Henry replied.

He's loyal. Got to give him that, Chris thought. "How much do you know?"

Henry smiled. "I know you are murderers. And the enemy."

"Wrong," Jessie said. "These people are harmless unless attacked."

"Jessie here was in the first attack on our island," Chris explained.

"Then she's a traitor!" Henry yelled.

Jessie slammed her fist into his injured shoulder.

"I fight for what's right!" she yelled back. "I betray only those who betray me."

"Do you know what you're even fighting for?" Chris asked Henry but received no answer. "Let's show him," he said to Jessie.

She called someone in to push Henry's wheelchair. Chris and Henry were rolled outside onto a lookout that commanded a view over most of the island.

"That is what you are fighting for," Chris stated, motioning to all the destroyed vessels on the shoreline.

"You deserved everything you got," Henry spat.

The Hidden Island

This guy won't give in. Chris painfully wheeled himself closer.

"We were attacked unprovoked. For money," Chris said. "This island produces a fuel that brings in millions of dollars every year. People come here to start new lives. The island to them is safety, hope, life. We're completely independent with our own education system, agriculture, and various other industries that make life here possible. The US tried to take that from us."

There was no response from Henry verbally but Chris could tell he was getting to him.

"They tried to shoot me down," Jessie said angrily. "Me. One of their own F16s. No remorse, no nothing. Just greed. Greed."

"You were a pilot?" Henry asked.

Chris knew he had him now. "I like you, Henry, for some reason, so I'm going to give you a chance. You can either be imprisoned for life or you can serve in the Serenidad military."

Henry remained silent for several moments. "One condition. The aircraft I flew in on. It has to be rescued and brought to me."

Chris sighed heavily. Pilots really did love their aircraft.

"If she's returned to me, then and only then will I serve with you."

Chris noticed the smile on Jessie's face. "How do we know it's not a trap?" he asked.

"It's not. I'll give you the codes. Very few people knew of this mission.

They probably think I'm dead right now anyway."

"Very well. Bring him to a room. Make him comfortable," Chris ordered.

When everyone had left, Jessie kissed Chris on the cheek. "Reminds me of when you turned me," she said, then hugged him.

"I knew where your plane was. I don't know where his is."

"I'm sure he knows," Jessie replied.

Chris was about to say something when Russell came up the ramp toward them.

"Chris. You'll never guess what just washed up on shore."

Chris hoped it was Henry's plane.

"A US life raft. It's been shot up."

"Didn't they rescue that tanker crew?"

"So we thought, but..."

"Should we send out the salvage ship?" Jessie suggested. "To make sure they're safe?"

Chris didn't like the idea but it was the right thing to do.

"She's right," Russell said. "If we find bodies we'll have to give them to the US. Right?"

"I don't want them anywhere near the island until I'm back on the *Magenta*," Chris stated firmly.

"Agreed. Last thing I want is another incident."

On board the MV Shattered Gold

Head of Security, Dean Blouin, walked onto the Bridge of the *MV Shattered Gold*. The ship, on loan to him and the rest of the crew, was being used in salvage efforts after the Great Battle. The islanders had made many modifications to render the ship battle-ready to ensure their location was as protected as possible. There were no Americans on board and Dean and his crew were monitoring all communications between the island people and the rest of their world. The Captain was sitting in his chair sipping on a cup of something hot. No one was ever privy to knowing what exactly was in the Captain's cup.

"This is crazy," Dean said. "It's like looking for a needle in a hay stack."

"We have our orders," the Captain said calmly. "The American told us where to find the aircraft."

"Who says it hasn't drifted? And what if the Americans have sent reinforcements?" Dean was angry.

"They will not. We are guaranteed that by the—"

"By the American?" Dean threw back his head and laughed. "We're risking our lives so that some American can have his damn plane back?" Dean waited for a response but got none. "I think you've forgotten what happened two years ago!"

That seemed to do it. The Captain rose from his seat and glared at

Dean. The Bridge went silent.

"Don't you dare go there!" The Captain stabbed the air with his forefinger. "I was one of the few survived that battle. My ship was hit in the bow. Only three of us made it out of that. I watched as my ship sank. I watched the damn Americans kill our own people. Do you think I'd be here if I wasn't bloody well sure this guy isn't lying?"

Despite himself, Dean took a step backwards.

"Now get back to your position."

Silently cursing, Dean made his way to the bow where he looked out at the ocean through binoculars. About two kilometers out was an odd black shape and as the distance decreased the shape took on form. "I'll be damned."

It was some sort of black aircraft floating on what appeared to be gray airbags. "Get the crane ready!" he shouted then returned his gaze to the strange aircraft just in time to see a muzzle flash coming from it. He ducked as an explosion erupted above him. He swung his pistol out over the rail and fired but his bullets never seemed to impact the aircraft. It fired again, this time causing an explosion at the MV *Shattered Gold*'s stern. Suddenly a loud high-pitched screech filled the air. The digital security personnel device on Dean's belt was shaking. Dean released it and tossed it overboard seconds before it exploded. He swung his gun out once more and finally was able to see the cockpit. What he saw made his throat go dry.

"Hold your fire! The American's telling the truth!" he shouted into the radio pinned to his shoulder. He then switched the radio's frequency to the one the American had supplied. Another explosion erupted, this time at the mid-section.

"Alpha, Charley, Delta, Zulu!" The gunshots and high-pitched screeching ceased immediately and the aircraft's flashing landing lights blinked on.

Dean called out the rest of the code: "Tango, Delta, Yankee, Golf."

"Who are you?" The female voice coming from the radio startled Dean.

"Um. That's not important," Dean said, still stunned.

An explosion erupted above him. "But it is important," the voice said.

"Dean Blouin. I am Head of Security of the *MV Shattered Gold*. I'm also a friend of your boss. That would be Henry. He wants you to come with us." Dean was unsure of what might happen.

"State second verification code," the voice said sternly.

Dean pulled a piece of paper from his pocket and read the number. "One, zero, nine, two, nine, two, three, four, eight, four, eight, two, nine, eight, three, seven, four, three."

The aircraft's landing lights were flashing again. The airbags supporting the aircraft expanded and what looked like a tube rose from its back. Everything soon lifted off the water and glided sideways until it was hovering over the deck of the *MV Shattered Gold.* Long landing gear extended from the belly and it touched down on the deck. The tube retracted into the aircraft's back and the aircraft flashed its landing lights four times.

Dean moved closer but the lights turned red so he thought it best not to get any closer. He returned to the edge of the deck and then depressed the transmit button on his radio.

"OK. It's on board. Now let's get outta here before anything else happens."

Serenidad

Henry had only recently been able to walk and enjoyed the views on the island. Despite his first impressions, he had grown to love it. It truly was impressive. These people had a place unknown to most of the world and had everything one needed. Housing, work, protection, food... It was all here. Henry could see himself living here. He had no one back home, his parents were dead, he was an only child and he had no sweetheart back in the US. *Plus* the US had sent him on a suicide mission. Most importantly, the island had saved the *Sparrow.* He had worked so hard to keep her flying, he would have hated to lose her. He stumbled over a rock. Pain shot through his wounds like fire, reminding him that he wasn't fully healed yet.

"Stupid rock," he muttered as he continued down the road toward the airstrip. He was wearing his knife combat gear and although it had been perfectly comfortable when he was healthy, it was painful right now. He had removed the two lower knives on the chest harness because they rubbed against the wound on his abdomen.

Henry's heart leaped when he saw his XM-89 *Sparrow* in the hangar and he quickened his pace but it still took him far too long to reach the hangar. A guard drew his weapon as Henry approached.

Hand extended, the guard said politely, "I'm sorry, sir, this is a restricted area."

Better than I would have gotten back in the US, Henry thought. "I have clearance."

Only then did the guard seem to notice Henry's combat gear. "You're the one that attacked Chris."

"That's behind us now," Henry said. It wasn't a complete lie. Henry and Chris were friends now but there was still understandable tension between them when it came to the attack. Henry was glad he hadn't killed the man but was also beating himself up for failing at his mission.

"Very well. ID?"

"Nope. Don't have any." He hadn't carried any with him on the mission. "I can easily get it though."

"Get it then," the guard prompted.

With that, the canopy to the *Sparrow* began to rise.

The guard shot a look at Henry. "We've been trying to open that since we got it here. How'd you do that?"

"I unlocked it," Henry said, holding up his communicator. When he neared the side of the aircraft, its ladder flipped down. He climbed in and reached for a plastic envelope.

"Sir. ID, please," the guard insisted.

"I just opened this aircraft. You really need my ID?"

"Procedures, sir."

Henry rolled his eyes and handed the ID card to the guard.

The guard glanced at it briefly before handing it back to Henry.

"Sorry for the inconvenience, sir." With that, he was back outside the hangar.

Henry turned the *Sparrow's* avionics on and went through the verification process.

"Welcome back, Henry," the computer said.

Henry breathed a sigh of relief. *Finally, a familiar voice.*

"Status of the mission?"

"Failed," Henry said. "When was the last communication with the United States?"

"Immediately following the drop."

Henry could call home right now and leave but he didn't want to. For some bizarre reason, he wanted to help this island. "Cease all communication with United States of America," he ordered.

"Reason?"

"Program compromised," Henry replied.

The computer beeped in acknowledgement. "Communication ceased."

"New mission," Henry stated.

"Mission parameters?"

"Protection of the Serenidad Island. We now serve with them."

"Mission set. Would you like me to change our default air force?"

"Change to Serenidad Air Force and Navy."

The computer beeped and displayed the service record for Henry to see.

"Threat detected," the computer called. "Target one-hundred-and-fifty feet, carrying a 9 mm weapon on his right hip."

"Chris is no longer a threat," Henry said and then climbed out of the *Sparrow.*

"Henry, I see you found your plane," Chris said limping over. Jessie was with him.

"You guys have taken good care of her," Henry replied.

"I need your help."

"What do you need?"

"We've recovered the bodies of the tanker crew that flew in with you a while back. We can ID three as crew but there's nothing on the others."

"Let's see 'em."

In the main town at the investigation building, they boarded an elevator that took them down into the basement.

"Why the patches, Henry?" Jessie asked.

Henry glanced at the dark grey patches on his black combat gear. "That's where your boyfriend shot me."

Chris chuckled. "You attacked first," he said as the elevator doors slid open into a cold room with two sheeted bodies lying on gurneys. Chris pulled the sheet away from one of them and Jessie did the same with the other body.

Henry recognized the one closest to Chris. "That one's my old CO's assistant, but this one I don't know. Where are their clothes?"

"Over there," said Chris. "Flight gear, looks like."

Henry picked through the garments.

"We know he was a pilot but his gear didn't match the others."

Henry noticed that the man's wings were missing. He went through the pockets of the gear.

"What are you doing?" Jessie asked.

"His wings aren't here. Could be lost or... Ah. Here we go." He pulled set of gold wings from a pocket.

Chris and Jessie looked at Henry, clearly confused.

"Did you always wear your wings, Jessie?" Henry asked.

"In uniform, yeah, but I had a stitch-on set when I flew."

"Me, too," said Henry. "And I carry my pins with me for good luck. This set of wings is for *Marine One*. This guy must be the pilot of *Marine One*."

Jessie shook her head. "So that so-called rescue chopper was just dumping bodies."

Chris turned to leave.

"You *are* going to tell the US about this right?" Henry said.

Chris stopped in his tracks but said nothing.

"Someone might be posing as this guy. He could try and kill the

President for all we know. You have to warn them."

"Unless this directly affects Serenidad and the safety of its people, I don't have to do anything," Chris said, his voice cold as ice.

"Don't you owe them, Chris? I mean they gave you a salvage ship, for crying out loud."

Chris turned on Henry. His eyes were filled with rage. "I owe the US nothing!" he shouted. "They attacked us! Slaughtered my men! Killed my sister! Threatened the lives of every single person on this island! They are nowhere near repaying the damage they have caused."

"You—"

"I do not want to hear it. The United States can burn to the ground, for all I care."

On board the *Magenta,* one year later

"Chris. Chris. Wake up."

Chris woke up to Henry shaking him and instinctively reached for his gun and pointed it but Henry grabbed his arm and twisted it until he dropped the gun.

"What's wrong?" Henry demanded handing the gun back to Chris.

Behind Henry, Chris could see four armed guards. Henry had his entire knife combat equipment on.

"Chris! What happened?" Henry shook him once more.

"I need some air," Chris said as he pushed past the group out of his room and to the ship's railing. He watched the waves crash against the *Magenta*'s side.

Henry followed. "Chris?"

"Bad dream," was all Chris said.

"I'll say. You put the whole boat on alert with your shouting. What were you dreaming about?"

"My first kill." A big wave hit the *Magenta,* sending up a spray that hit him square in the face.

"I have dreams about that kind of stuff, too, but I don't put a whole warship on alert when I have one," Henry said, trying to lighten the mood.

"I was thirteen." Henry was about to say something but Chris added. "Someone hired a hit man to take away what my best friend's dad loved as a way of getting back at him for ruining his life. The hit man took a shot at my best friend. He hit him in the arm and I shot back but missed. The hit man came around and shot my friend in the head. I put three rounds into the man's chest. After that, my uncle—lived on this island—decided that my family should join him. Now here I am commanding a killing machine." Chris sighed. "At least I won't miss this time."

After a few moments of silence between them, Henry said, "Don't mind me asking but what did you do to make the US so angry with you?"

Chris shrugged. It had been almost a year since Henry had first been ordered to kill Chris. They had inflicted almost identical wounds on each other. Chris believed the reason for this was because they were evenly matched and neither of them had had any real urge to kill each other. Since that time, Henry had perfected his knife-combat skills and was now working on board the *Magenta* as First Officer. Chris knew it would be only a matter of time before Henry would ask that question. He was surprised it had taken him this long. "The last time I saw the President, the Secretary of Defense— name was Fredrick Hurley—pulled a gun on him. I shot Hurley before he could shoot the President." Chris watched Henry's face turn white as flour. "What now, Henry?"

"I'm going to contact my old boss, General Blume. I think I know what happened."

"We'll ensure that you can't be tracked, but make it quick," Chris said as he pulled a satellite phone from his pocket then radioed the Communications officer to inform him of Henry's intentions. Chris handed the SAT phone to Henry who stepped out of hearing distance.

When Henry turned away, Chris inserted an earpiece into his ear.

"Henry! I thought you were dead!" came the voice of a man Chris assumed was General Blume.

"Look. I need to make this quick. Do you know who issued that hit on the Island commander?"

Chris heard rustling on the other end of the line. "The current Secretary of Defense. Dalton Murree."

"Thanks, Thomas. I have to go."

"What? Wait. No. We need to organize a rescue mission. Get you home. Where are—?"

"No, you don't. I'll figure out a way to fill you in later." The line went dead.

Chris turned slightly to slide his earpiece out and tuck it back into his pocket in one smooth move as Henry returned to hand back the SAT phone.

"After the death of Secretary of Defense, Frederick Hurley, his step-brother, Dalton Murree—" Henry laughed. "We all called him Hurley Squared because of how similar he and his step-brother were and he hated it. Well, he took over the position. He's the one who issued the order to have you taken out. We need to do something."

Chris knew that Henry was about to ask that Americans come to the island. That was the last thing he wanted.

"The brothers shared more than a parent, I think," Henry said.

"I told you when we found the tanker crew that unless it affects the island directly, we stay out of it."

"It affects the island, all right," Henry countered. "And in a bad way."

Chris was puzzled.

"If Dalton Murree manages to kill the President, he's in a position to make it look as if you did it. Get it? If that happens, all bets are off. Any peace you had with the US disappears."

Henry was right. Why did he have to be right? "Damn it, Henry."

White House Situation Room

"Sir," a presidential aide said, interrupting the Secretary of Defense's briefing. "Urgent call for you."

The President motioned for the assistant to approach.

The assistant whispered something to the President whose face drained of color.

"The meeting is adjourned. General Blume, stay here with me," the President said.

Thomas Blume watched as all the men and women filed out of the room. The screen at the front of the room lit up with the image of a man, tall with powerful eyes and a heavy five-o'clock shadow.

"Russell. How nice to see you again," the President said.

"I must say the same to you, Mr. President. I would like to congratulate you on your second term. And who is this?"

"General Thomas Blume and unfortunately, that's all I can tell you."

"Happy to see you're holding up your end of our arrangement," the man replied.

Thomas's mind was racing. Who is this man? And what are they talking about?

"As I'm sure you are aware," the man said, "last year we shot down one of your KC-10 tankers because it did not turn back when warned. Before you say anything, we know it was attended by an armed fighter, otherwise we probably would have intercepted it rather than destroy it."

The President nodded.

"We recovered the bodies of those crew members and discovered some disturbing information. We thought you would like to hear it. Perhaps recover these bodies for their grieving families. Surely they've waited long enough."

"You are very much right," the President said.

"Good. Take *Marine One* to the coordinates that are being printed as we speak."

At that moment, the printer in the east corner of the room came to life. *How did they access our communication system? It's secure!*

"You will rendezvous with the salvage ship and you know who," the man finished.

That's when it hit Thomas. They were from the island that Henry had been sent to.

"Thank you, Russell. We'll see you in a few days," the President said.

"Just make sure to watch your men this time," the man said.

The President grunted and the screen went blank.

"Sir, you can't possibly go out to that island. You won't come back intact," Thomas said, forgetting his place.

"I've been there before. Besides, they won't let us near the shore—"

"Can't you send some else? Like an ambassador or someone like that?"

"I'm going myself because these people have the key to ruining the image of the United States of America. Not to mention my reputation as a politician."

"Very well, sir, but I must ask. Did you give them the codes for our communications system?" Thomas retrieved the paper from the printer's out tray.

"No. I was hoping you would have an explanation."

Sighing heavily, Thomas shook his head.

"That can't mean anything good."

"The *Sparrow* has access codes to all our communications systems so it can send emergency messages. Or check in with at us any time. If they've captured the aircraft... I don't want to think about what could happen if they've captured that aircraft."

"The more we improved that thing, the more of a problem it became. Come on, Thomas. Let's get moving. We don't want to be late."

On board the *Magenta*

"Sir, they're hovering over the salvage ship," Alex called across the Bridge.

"All right, lock 'em," Chris ordered. He walked over and watched the screen as the dots representing the helicopters scattered in an attempt to conceal which one was *Marine One*. Chris smiled as he noticed one was flying differently than the others were. He tuned the ship's radio and hit the microphone button. *You guys aren't that smart you know*, he thought while cueing his microphone. "I know exactly which one of you is *Marine One*."

"How do you know that?" someone said over the radio.

Chris instantly knew who it was. "That's easy, General Blume. Or do you prefer Thomas?"

Chris motioned for Ian to surface the vessel and then moved out of the Bridge and down the hall reaching the stern just as *Marine One* was landing on the make-shift floating landing pad that was being towed behind the *Magenta*. The President, General Blume, Secretary of Defense Dalton Murree and two Secret Service men climbed out.

"Leave it to you to find a flaw in what we thought to be the perfect system," the President said as he climbed onto the ship.

"Welcome back, Mr. President," Chris said.

"Thank you. Now where are we meeting?"

"Below decks again, but first, look to the sky." Chris pointed to a black dot off in the distance that was rapidly growing larger.

Within seconds, the *Sparrow* passed overhead. It continued out past the ship before shooting into a near vertical climb and circling back. It slowed and hovered over the *Magenta*'s deck.

"It took us forever to train a pilot to be that good. How did you do it in just one year?" Obviously impressed, the President gazed up at the belly of the aircraft.

"That's easy," Chris said as the aircraft rolled open its canopy. The pilot leaped from the cockpit and landed on his feet on the deck. "*We* didn't."

Chris enjoyed the look on the US officers' faces as Henry took his helmet off. Henry snapped to attention and saluted. "Greetings, Mr. President, Mr. Secretary, General Blume. Please follow us."

The men walked to a door and Thomas tapped Chris on the shoulder. Both Chris and Henry turned to talk to him.

"Henry said you'd explain what happened a year ago," Thomas said.

Chris filled Thomas in as to what had happened when Henry attacked him.

"There's not much more to it," Chris said and walked through the open door. He stopped one of the Secret Service men. "You wait here." He allowed the second man into the conference room where he showed them to their seats. A projector extended from the ceiling revealed the on-screen images of five dead men.

"Russell was unable to attend our little meeting and sends his regrets. There was a matter on the island that needed his attention. Now these three..." Chris said pointing to three of the men, "... are the KC-10 crew. And these two are men I can't identify."

"But I can," Henry said pointing to the first of the two unidentified men. "This is the former pilot for *Marine One*. And this one is Thomas's former aide."

Chris spoke. "Now for the reason we brought you here. Henry?"

Henry nodded and threw two knives at Secretary of Defense Murree pinning his clothing to his chair. The Secret Service agent whom Chris had allowed on the ship stepped toward Henry. Chris raised his pistol, shook his head.

"This man—your Secretary of Defense, of all people," Henry growled. "—is the one who authorized the assassination attempt on Chris."

Murree laughed nervously. "Ridiculous. Mr. President, tell them to remove these knives immediately."

Henry grabbed Murree's pistol and tossed it to Chris. Chris grabbed it, removed one shell and smiled.

"The bullets we extracted from the bodies had an imperfection in them, caused by a damaged magazine," Chris said, examining the bullet. "This one looks like it could be a match. Why would he kill these men, you might ask? Well," Chris smiled. "We think he might try the same thing his brother failed to do."

Murree laughed again. "So, say I *am* planning whatever you think I'm planning. What are you going to do about it? Kill me?"

"Trust me, if we wanted you dead, those knives would be in your head not in your uniform," Henry snapped.

"There are things worse than death." Chris placed Murree's gun on the table at the front of the room. As Henry bent to change the image on the projection screen, Murree threw himself at the two men. As if rehearsed, both men swung around and kicked him in the gut sending him flying across the room.

Chris's radio beeped. He pressed the acknowledge button.

"Alpha Charlie Tango," was all that came across. Chris frowned at the battle station code.

We have to get everyone to the helicopters," Chris shouted and shot the Secret Service agent standing in the corner then ran out of the conference room, Henry at his side. As they turned the corner, they were welcomed by a barrage of bullets. He turned and nodded to Henry. Henry climbed onto a ledge and unscrewed an air vent. Chris swung out and fired at the intruders. One fell, but a bullet just missed Chris's lower left leg, tearing the fabric of his pants. Then Henry, looking more like a black flash, fell from the ceiling and the two intruders left standing, fell.

The black figure stabbed the last man and shouted. "Let's go!"

"Good job, Henry," Chris said as they ran down the hall. They made it out to the deck and saw the pilot of *Marine One* with a rifle.

"Get down!" Henry shouted and threw a knife. The blade hit the pilot in the left shoulder and she retreated to the chopper. Soon the VOTL aircraft's blades were up to speed. Then Chris heard the click of a hammer.

"You should have kept my gun," Murree said.

Chris spun, grabbed Murree's gun and punched him. Murree dropped his gun and ran for the chopper. Chris shot him in the foot but Murree kept dragging himself toward the chopper. By now, the other choppers were in the air. *Marine One* lifted off the floating landing pad and joined the circling pattern.

Henry yelled "Now!"

A high-pitched whine pierced the air and two of the helicopters exploded startling Chris. "What the—?"

"Murree put explosives on the two escort helicopters," Henry yelled over the noise of the *Magenta's* guns. Ammunition ripped into the sky but missed the fleeing helicopter.

"I'm going after him," Henry called and ran out to the *Sparrow.* Within seconds she lifted off the salvage ship alongside the *Magenta.*

Then someone knocked Chris to the floor.

On board *Sparrow 1*

"Target two miles out. Be careful," the computer said as it popped the canopy.

Henry jumped out grabbing the portside wheel well of the former *Marine One*. He pulled himself up and jacked the door to the open position. He swung in and kicked Secretary of Defense Murree to the floor. He ran to the front and closed the door just as the pilot was raising her weapon. The chopper suddenly dove, knocking Henry off his feet. He regained his footing as the chopper returned to level flight. Murree came at Henry swinging. Henry grabbed Murree's fist and flipped him to the floor. Murree grunted, clearly in pain, as Henry kicked him in his shot foot.

"You should have thought twice before using me," Henry said angrily.

Murree pulled himself to his feet but Henry punched him again and down he went.

"That's for using me," Henry spat. A knife extended from the toe of his boot and he kicked Murree in the shin. "And that's for using the *Sparrow.*"

Murree screamed out in pain. "Didn't think you'd fail. Or be this smart for that matter." Murree grunted, spitting blood onto the floor.

Henry pulled his nitro knife from a back pocket. He turned it on and threw it at Murree. As it imbedded itself into Murree's chest its plunger depressed.

Patrick Gloutney

"At least you'll go out with a bang," Henry said as he threw himself down to roll out the door onto the hovering *Sparrow* below.

On board *Marine One*

Renée kicked the door but it wouldn't open. Frustrated she shot the lock off and pushed the door open to see Murree clutching at his chest. She could see something green sticking out of him.

"Sir!" she called.

Then a blue spark shot out from the green object and Murree exploded.

Renée was sent flying into the controls causing the chopper to dive once again. When she pulled herself up she could tell she had worsened the injury to her bad arm but she didn't care. The chopper had begun to spin. She grabbed the controls with her good arm and tried to stop the spin. Every warning light in the cockpit was flashing. The one that caught her attention was the TAIL ROTOR DAMPER FAILURE message on the main instrument panel.

"I should have shot him as soon as I met him," she muttered to herself as she cut the main engine. The former *Marine One* slammed into the ocean seconds later.

When Renée came to, she was lightheaded and found it a tiresome task to move. She reached up to wipe moisture off her forehead but when she brought her hand back down it was covered with blood. Water was sloshing into the dying helicopter. The main instrument panel was coated with blood. She must have hit her head on the panel on impact. She quickly assessed her situation and came to an obvious conclusion.

Not wanting to face a judge for what she had done and having no to family to go home to, she drew her sidearm. Placing it on her chest over her heart, she fired.

On board the *Magenta*

Chris punched William and he fell to the floor. William was Russell's cousin and by Russell's request, Chris had trained him to fight. William jumped up and got Chris in the side. Chris punched William in the throat before getting a punch to the face. Chris managed to regain his footing but could feel blood trickling off his lip.

"You learned well," Chris said, resting his hand on his empty holster. His gun had slid overboard at the beginning of the fight. The US officials had retreated below decks after Chris was first knocked down.

Typical, he thought before ducking to avoid yet another punch from William. Chris grabbed William's fist and flipped him. He reached for his knife only to realize that William had somehow gotten hold of it and was now in the process of throwing it overboard.

"Not bad, but do you remember the first thing I taught you?" Chris asked.

"Never think you have the upper hand."

"That's correct," Chris said as he grabbed the gun on William's belt. He raised it and fired three shots at William's chest but nothing happened. He opened the magazine to examine a bullet. "Blanks?"

William grabbed Chris by the head and flipped him onto the floor, ripping the gun from Chris's hands in the process.

"Not all of them." A shot rang out and Chris felt the bullet impact his skin. The whole world seemed to slow down. He could hear the *Sparrow* flying overhead and William laughing. He tried to move but couldn't. After what seemed like an eternity he heard someone call out.

"Chris!" Seconds later two knives appeared in William, one in his chest and the other in his head. Henry soon appeared above Chris.

"It's a good thing he was not a better shot," Chris said as Henry pulled a strip of cloth from his pocket and bandaged up Chris's shoulder.

"I'd have to agree with that."

Henry helped Chris to his feet and they made their way below decks where the US officials all wore terrified expressions.

"Chris, are you okay?" the President asked.

"I'll live. But I suggest you be more selective when you pick your officers. This is the second time my military has had to kill one of them."

"I would hope to prevent any future mishaps," the President said. "If Henry would like, I propose that he stay with you as a liaison officer. He will be able to contact me and any other member of our government twenty-four-seven."

Henry nodded and Chris smiled.

"So when will *Marine One* pick us up?" Thomas asked from behind the group.

"It won't be. I shot it down," said Henry. "You needed a new one anyway."

The crowd let out a worried chuckle.

"The salvage ship will take you back to the United States," Chris said, his smile broadening.

"Thank you, again, Chris. And please accept my personal apologies for this major mishap." The President shook Chris's hand.

"Just imagine what will happen when you finish your second term."

As the President exited, all but Chris and Henry followed him.

"You could have gone home you know," Chris told Henry.

"Yeah, I know. But it's more fun here. Just one thing, though. How did you know I got Murree?"

"Because if you hadn't, you'd still be out there chasing him down. Even if it meant crashing yourself."

The two friends reached the Bridge just as the salvage ship was pulling away.

Chris took his seat at the center of the Bridge.

"All right, Ian. Take us home."

Patrick Gloutney

Acknowledgments

I would like to acknowledge the contributions of Sharyn Heagle who provided moral and technical support along with knowledge to which I would not otherwise have had access. Without her, this book would not have been possible. Thanks to Sherrill Wark of Crowe Creations who, as well as acting as my editor, provided valuable insight into how to proceed with the publication of my manuscript. Finally, I would like to thank my family who stood behind me and put up with the process of my writing this manuscript. Thanks to you all.

Patrick Gloutney

Patrick Gloutney was born in Amherst Nova Scotia and moved to Ottawa Ontario in 2012. He is the recipient of awards ranging from community involvement to public speaking including the Osgoode Township High School Trustees' Award in 2014 and second place winner of the Canadian Authors Association Nation Capital Youth Writing Contest in 2013. When he's not writing he's attending school or running his company, Stonecroft Yard Work and Odd Jobs, playing music, helping organize school teams and events, or attending Cadet Training.

https://sites.google.com/site/patrickgloutney/

www.ingramcontent.com/pod-product-compliance
Lightning Source LLC
Chambersburg PA
CBHW031956170626
46807CB00006B/2515